Dragon Boats

Dragon Boats

A CELEBRATION

Pat Barker

RAINCOAST BOOKS
Vancouver

Copyright © 1996 by Pat Barker

All rights reserved. No part of this publication may be reproduced or transmitted in any form or by any means, electronic or mechanical, including photocopying, recording, or by any information storage and retrieval system, now known or to be invented, without permission in writing from the publisher.

First published in 1996 by

Raincoast Book Distribution Ltd.
8680 Cambie Street
Vancouver, B.C.
V6P 6M9
(604) 323-7100

1 3 5 7 9 10 8 6 4 2

CANADIAN CATALOGUING IN PUBLICATION DATA

Barker, Pat, 1960–
Dragon boats

ISBN 1-55192-008-5

1. Dragon boat racing. 2. Dragon boats – Design and construction.
3. Dragon boat festival. I. Title.
GV786.B37 1996   796.1'4   C95-911100-X

Designed by Dean Allen
Edited by Michael Carroll

Printed and bound in Hong Kong

*To the memory of my mother,
Doreen Elizabeth Barker (1931–1994).
She was the strongest person I've ever known.*

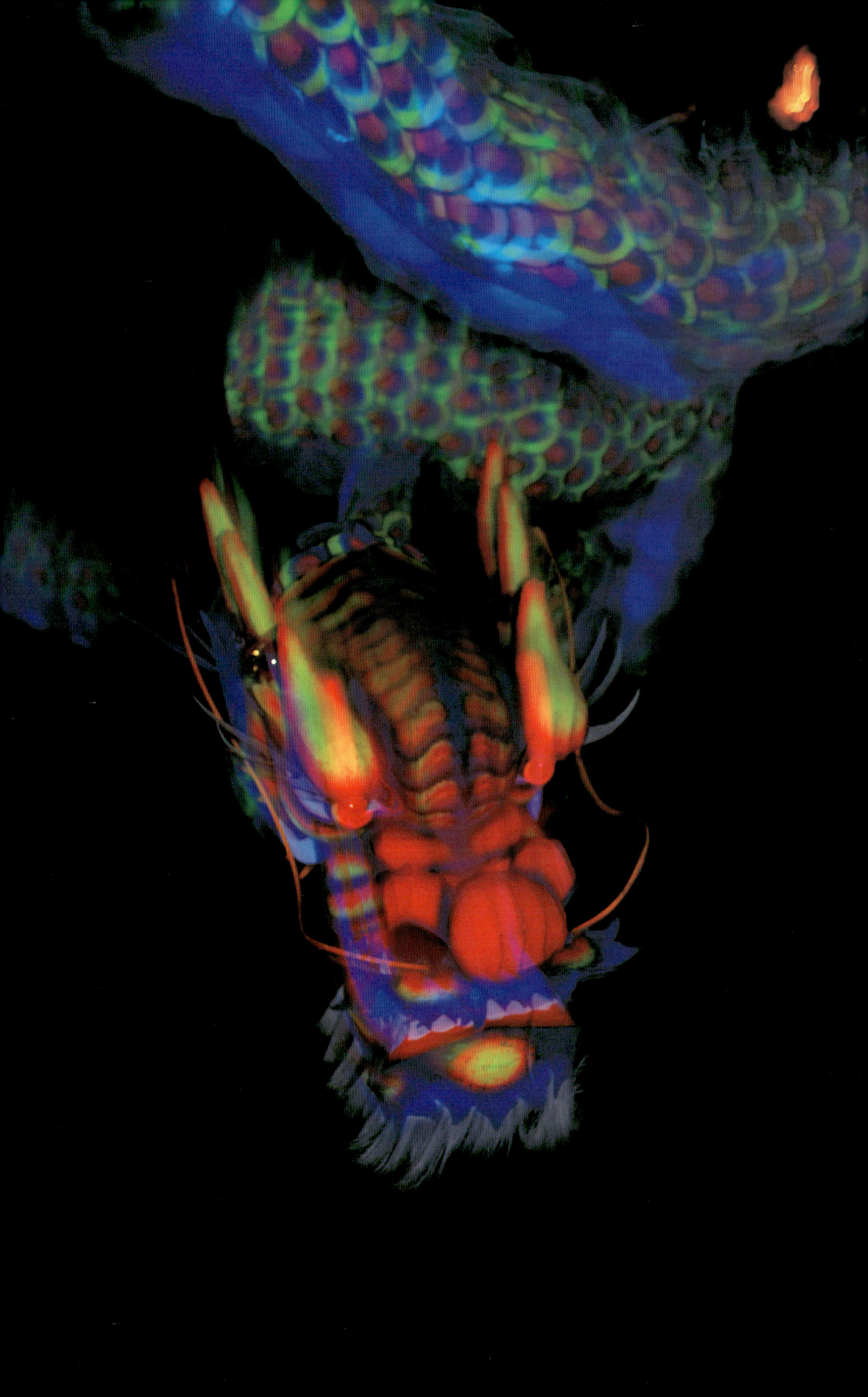

Contents

Foreword *ix*

Preface *xiii*

1 High Noon in China: Dragon Boat Origins and Culture *1*

    Dragons Through the Ages 18

2 Shaping the Dragon: Boats and Builders *21*

    Figureheads Past and Present 36

3 Paddles Up!: Races and Racers *39*

    White Light, Power Animals, and Wu *63*

4 Delighting the Senses: Festivals and Races Around the World *67*

    Yueyang and the Buddha's Laughter 99

5 A Glorious Future: Dragon Boat Fever in the Next Millennium *103*

Glossary *113*

Bibliography *117*

Illustration Credits *121*

Dragon dance performed at closing ceremonies of 1995 Hong Kong Dragon Boat Festival.

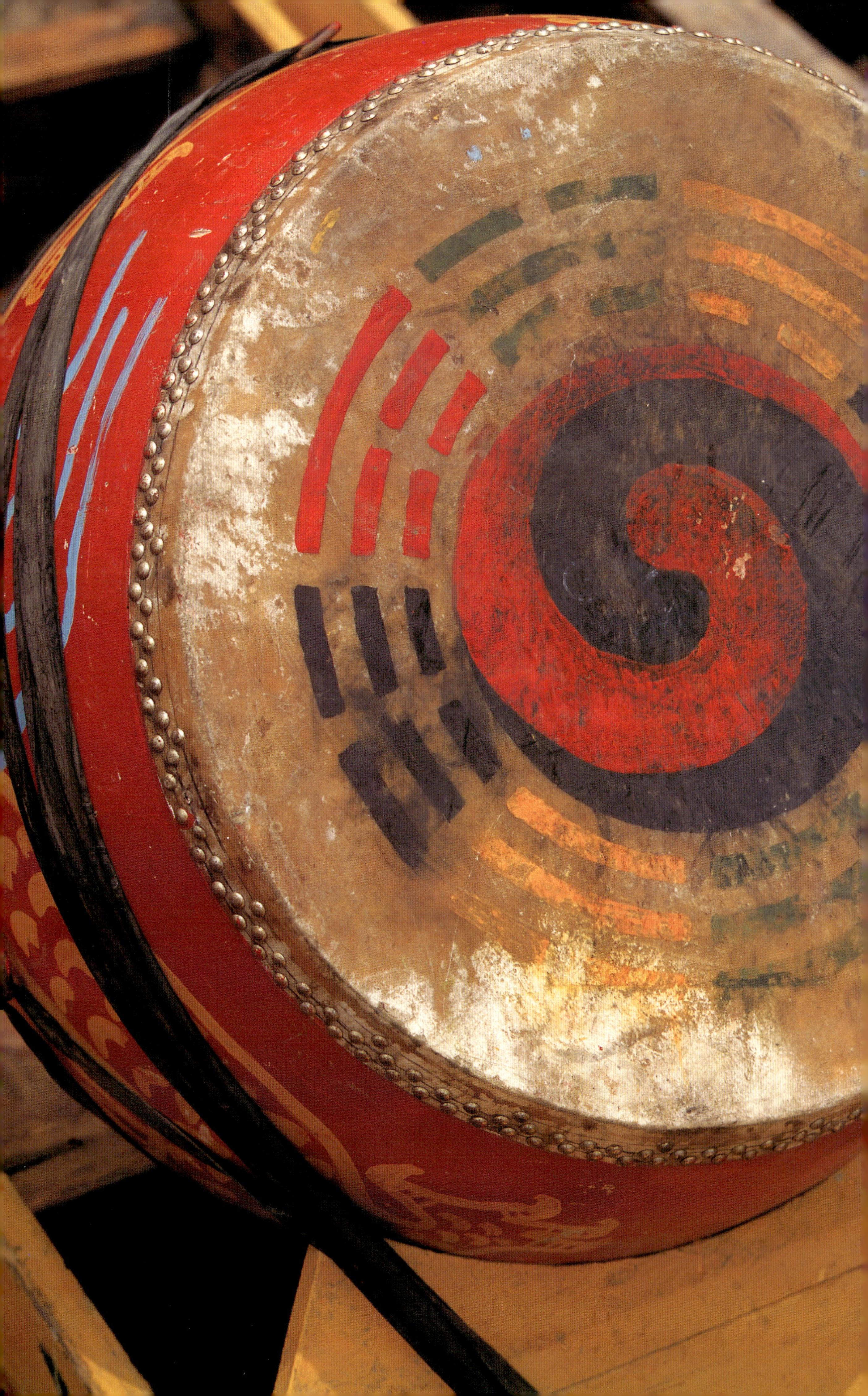

Foreword

THE BEAT OF THE DRUM, the size of the colorful boats, the number of competitors in each crew, the speed of the boats as 20 paddles thrash through the water in unison, these are but some of the ingredients that make dragon boat racing that little bit different than other water sports. It is also a combination of facts that makes the sport exciting to take part in, to watch, and to write a book about.

Dragon boat racing is probably one of the fastest-growing sports in the world. It is full of ritual and ancient traditions that go back 2,000 years to a time of plots and intrigues in southern China, which culminated in the suicide by drowning of Qu Yuan in the Miluo River. The death of this great statesman poet has been commemorated ever since by the Chinese through their dragon boat festivals, which today attract more than 20 million participants in China alone. In recent years, through the initiative of the Hong Kong Tourist Association, this Chinese tradition has matured into a modern sport that is practiced in more than 30 countries worldwide. As executive president of the International Dragon Boat Federation (IDBF), which was founded as recently as 1991, it is particularly gratifying to be asked to write this foreword. The IDBF was formed to develop, organize, coordinate, represent, and guide the sport and, most important, to preserve the Chinese culture associated with it. This last objective clearly shows that the IDBF has a duty to support traditional dragon boat festivals around the world, not to change them, whilst adding a new dimension to their traditions by developing and promoting a modern sport.

The holding of the First World Championships for national crews in Yueyang, China, in June 1995, in which countries from five continents took part, was for me a landmark in this process and demonstrates that dragon boat racing, at the highest level, is every bit as competitive and serious as any other sport. Its strength, however, is at the other end of the sporting spectrum where novice competitors can take part in a race with the minimum of experience or training. It is this fun element

Detail of dragon boat drum in Yueyang, China.

HONG KONG
HONG
Amathus Dragon Boat Club
Fuzhou - China - 1988
Hamburg - Germany - 1989
Kreuzlingen - Switzerland - 1989
Mechelen - Belgium - 1990
Amsterdam - Holland - 1990
Mechelen - Belgium - 1991
Mechelen - Belgium - 1992
Vollendam - Holland - 1992
Yangtze - China - 1992
Schwerin - Germany - 1993
Belfast - Northern Ireland - 1993
Hamburg - Germany - 1994
J & R Frood Engineering
Dragon Boat Paddles
HONG
KONG

FOREWORD

of the sport on which festival organizers, national associations, and the IDBF itself must build, especially among young people, if dragon boat racing is to become the mass participation sport on water that I believe it is destined to be.

To help this process the IDBF has introduced two new international competitions – the annual World Cup, aimed at international race organizers, and the biannual World Club Crew Championships, designed to enhance established dragon boat festivals. Both competitions are intended to add that extra dimension to established events without adversely affecting their traditions. The First World Club Crew Championships will be held in Vancouver, Canada, in June 1996, with the World Cup coming on line at other international races during the year.

The final accolade for any sport is Olympic status, and the IDBF is already active in this direction, too, with an application for the recognition of dragon boat racing being put before the International Olympic Committee (IOC). Such recognition of a sport by the IOC does not mean automatic inclusion in the Olympic Games, but it is the first step, and one that must be made, if dragon boat racing is to reach the pinnacle of international sports.

MIKE HASLAM
Executive President
International Dragon Boat Federation
London, England

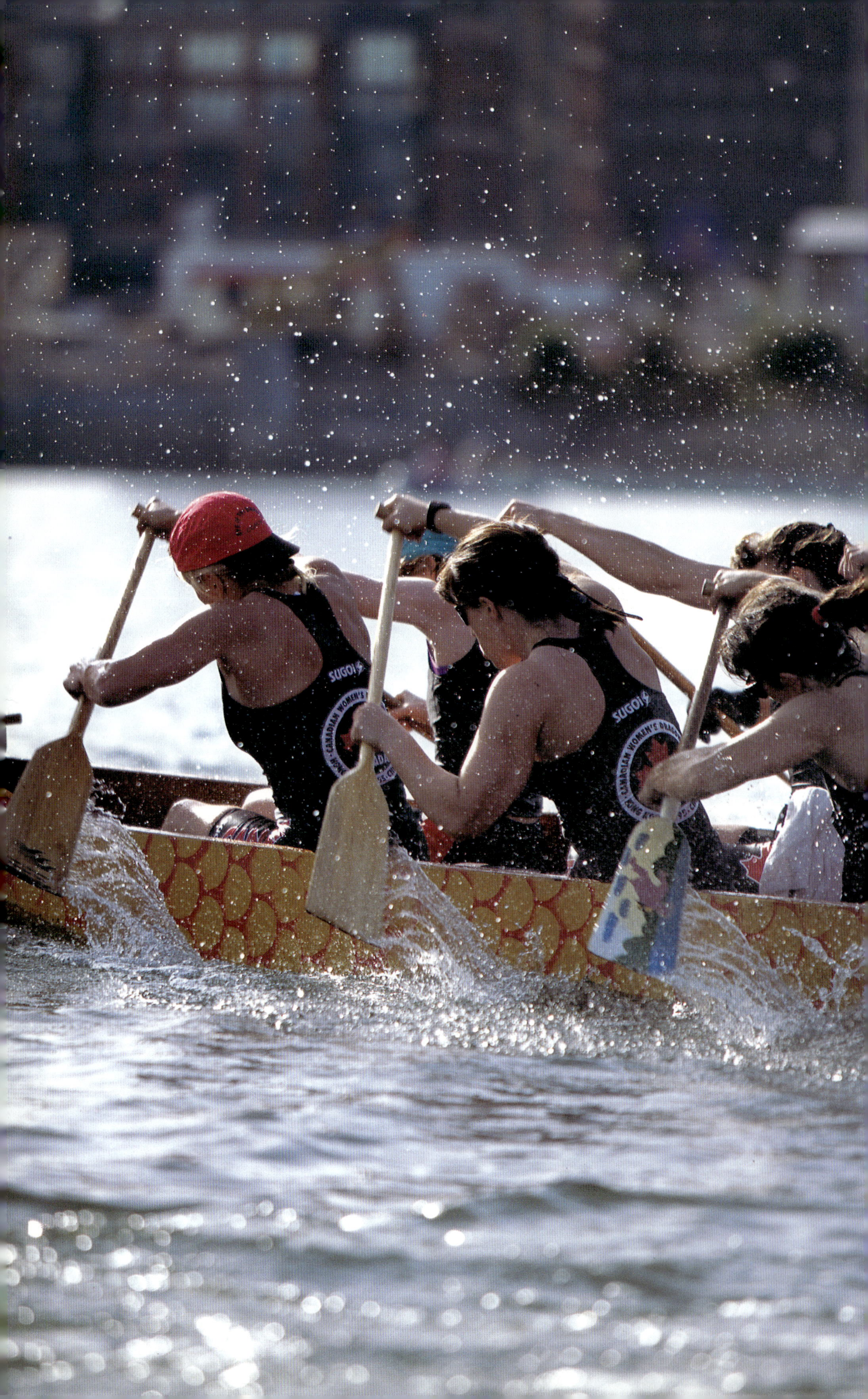
SUGOI

Preface

LIKE MOST DRAGON BOATERS, I was coaxed into paddling by a friend. In 1986 in Vancouver my friend, Alison Hart, and some other women were trying to form a dragon boat team that would become the first all-women's crew in Canada. Little did I know that this unusual ancient Chinese sport would consume nearly a decade of my life, both on and off the water. Dragon boating has the uncanny ability to draw large numbers of competitors and spectators and somehow keep them involved for many years.

The passion that envelopes a paddler isn't immediate, however. One must endure two to three weeks of sore muscles due to paddling on the same side. And then there are the cold, dark winter practices that seem to last an eternity. Maybe it was paddling in those conditions at first that made the later warm summer evenings of practice all the more special.

In 1987 I spent the winter and spring on a bicycle in Australia and New Zealand. It was here that I saw the beautiful and ornate boats of the Maori and was fortunate enough to be part of a war canoe celebration. Meanwhile, back home, the newly christened False Creek Women's Dragon Boat Team had found a coach by the name of Don Irvine, and there were rumors that the team would compete overseas. In 1988 we found ourselves on the start line in Hong Kong in our first international race. Nearly three minutes later we had defeated the team from Shun De, a district of Guangdong Province in the People's Republic of China. No non-Asian team had ever beaten them. Unfortunately for us it was just a heat, and Shun De paddled away with gold in the final race. Winning silver that year worked to our advantage, though, for it made us hungry for competition and made us even more excited about returning to Hong Kong.

I skipped the winter months in Vancouver again in 1989, but this time I traveled to a much colder place in a remote area of northern China where I coached a junior women's provincial cross-country ski

The celebrated False Creek Women's Dragon Boat Team going all out in a training session in Vancouver.

team. In the spring I returned in time to join the False Creek women's team for another unofficial world championship in Hong Kong. This time our team won gold. Other gold medals came in subsequent years, but Shun De reclaimed its title in 1991 when our team decided not to compete in Hong Kong. When we returned in 1992, however, we were triumphant once again. That would be my last race as a competitor in Hong Kong.

It was in the process of writing a treatment for a documentary film on dragon boating that this book came to be. I am truly indebted to my good friend Carol Sogawa, who gave me assistance and support on the project right from the beginning. I also send a wave of my paddle to Mark Stanton, Raincoast Books' president and publisher, for it was his vision and familiarity with developing sports that allowed him to see the potential of this book. And I thank Caroline Schroeder for pointing me in Raincoast's direction.

To Michael Carroll, managing editor of Raincoast, who coached me through the manuscript, I would like to send a "Penang-style drum roll." In his busy schedule Michael found the time to meet weekly, supply new deadlines, and ask the right questions. His expertise was invaluable in shaping the manuscript for this book. A creative flag wave must also go out to Dean Allen, Raincoast's art director, who patiently sifted through thousands of slides and pieces of art to design this book with great style. And thanks also go out to Carol Watterson, Raincoast's special sales manager, for her support.

To Paul Morrison, principal photographer of this book, I am indebted not only for his talents as a photographer, but also for his willingness to participate in the project on very short notice. I am also extremely grateful to photographer Rod Luey, who helped plant the seed for this book, and to photographer Yun Lam Li, who assisted in both photographs and fundraising. I would also like to thank photographers John Wertschek, Becky Armstrong, Ken A. Meisner, Wayne Asaoka, and Jeff Vinnick for their contributions.

Thanks go out to G. King Photo in Vancouver for its quality photographs and continued service, and to Lens and Shutter for sponsorship. I am forever indebted to the Jack Bell Foundation and RE/MAX Real Estate for believing in the concept of the book and for their generous donations. Cathay Pacific Airways and the Hong Kong Tourist Association, both founding sponsors of dragon boating in Vancouver and supporters of festivals around the world, made it possible for me to take a crew to China and Hong Kong. These two organizations have offered their continued support and sponsorship of dragon boating and have helped to establish it as one of the most popular new

PREFACE

sports in the world. I would also like to thank the Regal Kowloon and Hong Kong Renaissance Hotels for their service and outstanding accommodation. And I would like to thank Stephanie Gutherie of Communicaide Marketing Services in Toronto for corresponding with China and Hong Kong.

I would particularly like to thank Vincent Lo and Don Irvine of Six-Sixteen Dragon Boats Limited for their help with the manuscript, especially chapter 2. These two men have contributed a tremendous amount of their time to the sport of dragon boating – Vincent, as manager of the False Creek women's team, and Don, as its former coach. To Don I extend a personal thanks for his excellent coaching and motivating practices. Each practice seemed a little harder than the last. Coaches can have a great impact on a person's life, and although I've never told him, he changed the way I paddled the day he put his hand on my shoulder and said, "I know you can put more power into that paddle."

To Hugh Fisher, Olympian and visionary, and to Drew Mitchell of the Sport Medicine Council of British Columbia, both dedicated, committed coaches, I extend my thanks for their input into chapters 3 and 5. And I am forever indebted to Sam Carter and the Canadian International Dragon Boat Festival for the use of the dragon artifacts collection, and especially to Sam for his contributions to this book.

I would also like to send a special thanks to Mike Haslam in Britain for writing the foreword and for his help in chapter 4. In fact, I am indebted to all the people from various countries who contributed slides or information on international festivals and races, including Melinda Parsons, Joel Shilling, and Tom Meurlott in the United States; Marinna Millanta-Lowrey in New Zealand; Anne Watson in Australia; Howard Kwan in Canada; Benjamin R. Ramos, Jr., in the Philippines; Nicola Osse in South Africa; S. Essara of the Tourism Authority of Thailand; India's Tourist Office in Toronto; Mason Hung, Claire Lau, and Stephen Wong of the Hong Kong Tourist Association; and Katherine Lynch and Yan Yan Li also in Hong Kong.

There are numerous others who helped a great deal from the start of this project: Fiona Kennett and Lindsey Pollard, for their critical eye and their huge hearts; Sonny Wong and Ed Ng, organizers of the Canadian International Dragon Boat Festival; Adrian Lee, for sharing his expertise on dragon boating and for his generous reading of the manuscript; and the many members of the False Creek men's and women's teams, for their support and friendship all these years. And an extra special thanks to the Canadian Society of Asian Arts for their financial support and belief in this project.

Splashing at dragon boat races is an age-old custom. Here racers indulge with great abandon at the awards ceremony of the 1995 Hong Kong Dragon Boat Festival.

PREFACE

And there are still others who made contributions: Gail Morrison, Dario Baldasso, Michelle Salvador, Carlos Capdevila, Joan Barker, Katherine Neilsen, Andy Hale, Kathryn Reid, Elizabeth McQueen, Sarina McKenzie, Marilyn Cherenko, Larry Chu, Andrea Dillon, Mary Anne Purdy, Anne-Marie Nehring, Bob Solar, Anna Gibbs, Michael Maxwell, and Alison Hart. Oh, and I could never leave out my grade 13 physical education instructor from Ottawa, Robert Edwards, who introduced me to paddling some 17 years ago. The memories of those trips through Algonquin Park will stay with me always.

And last but not least I would like to thank my husband, Jim Solar, for letting me take the time off to write this book, for the extra attention he paid to our son, Nathan, and for the specification drawings of the dragon boats that grace chapter 2.

Paddles up! Take it away!

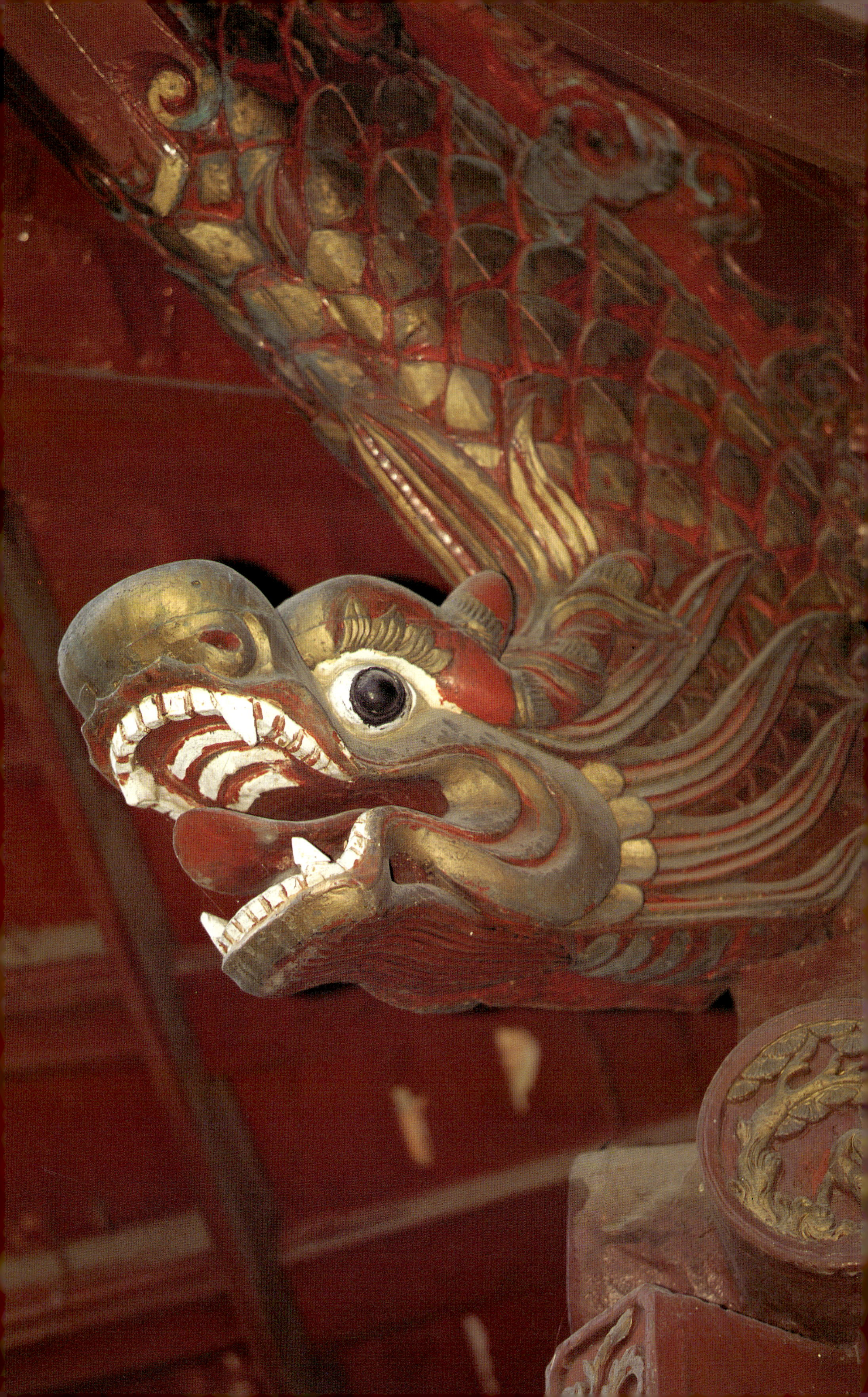

1 High Noon in China

Dragon Boat Origins and Culture

Perched on the bow behind a magnificent dragon head, the boat's drummer is exposed to the spray of 20 paddles, all of them reaching out toward her. Blinking away the salt water from her eyes, the drummer has become the heartbeat of the dragon. There is little space between the paddlers who have wedged themselves into awkward positions, yet somehow they make paddling on one side look deceptively easy. Each person becomes a silhouette of the next, their blades move up and down like pistons in the water. In the rear of the boat, balancing between a 20-foot oar and the open sea, the steersperson lifts the paddle slightly from one direction to the next, searching for that delicate balance.

Heaven's fire the bright sun burns,
Earth's fire the Earth to ashes turns.
But when Thunder's flame flashes far and wide,
The evil demons quickly hide.
By Thunder's flame now purified,
The boat may o'er the four seas ride.
  – Ancient Chinese Spell

UNTIL RECENTLY the ancient Chinese sport of dragon boat racing was unheard of within the non-Chinese community. Today it is one of the fastest-growing athletic events in the world. In fact, in 1998 special international dragon boat races will be held as a prelude to the Commonwealth Games in Penang, Malaysia. The International Dragon Boat Federation, headquartered in London, England, hopes this step will lead to the eventual incorporation of the sport in the Commonwealth Games, as well as inclusion as a demonstration sport in future Olympic Games.

Dragon boat racing owes much of its popularity to the dragon boat festival in Hong Kong, an event that has played host to international competition since 1976. Much of what is known about this unique sport has been handed down over the centuries, filtering through these races in Hong Kong. Hidden behind the popular legends of the festival, however, is a much darker side – a history enshrouded in fertility rites, superstitions, and human sacrifice.

Detail of a dragon carving, Yueyang Tower, China.

DRAGON BOATS: A CELEBRATION

Statue of Qu Yuan, Nanhu Stadium, Yueyang.

If one were to question local fishermen in China or Hong Kong about the history of the dragon boat festival, many stories would surface. Perhaps the most popular legend recounted would be that of Qu Yuan, a great patriot and poet who lived in China during the Warring States period (481–221 BC). This era was one of extraordinary political, economic, and social change. With only seven of the great feudal kingdoms remaining, it was a time of treachery and shifting alliances. The smaller and less resourceful states of Yan, Han, Zhao, and Wei depended on shrewd diplomacy to maintain a precarious autonomy. Military assistance was supplied to developing states to block possible takeovers by opposing states.

The larger, more powerful states of Qi in the northeast, Qin in the far west, and Chu in the south controlled vast tracts of land that were rich in resources and were capable of sustaining large armies. These larger states were known for their barbaric ways and were feared by all. Qin was particularly infamous for its brutal warfare and savagery. On one occasion, when Zhao troops had been divided by a strategic Qin maneuver, they surrendered on the trust that their lives would be spared. Instead, the Qin army slaughtered the 450,000 Zhao troops by burying them alive.

The state of Qin, determined to conquer Chu, drew up a fake treaty, which it encouraged the king of Chu to sign. Qu Yuan, one of the most trusted advisers in Chu, cautioned his king against signing the treaty. All of the states, regardless of their size, paid great heed to their political advisers. Men like Qu Yuan were employed to devise schemes to maintain the balance of power. They were men of great intellect and influence.

However, in an atmosphere of internal strife and struggles for status and control, Qu Yuan stood on dangerous ground. For all his good intentions, his advice was misinterpreted by the king, who saw it as an attempt to assume greater political power. As punishment, the king had Qu Yuan banished to a remote area of southern China in Hunan Province.

Qu Yuan spent the remaining years of his life in a state of depression, wandering aimlessly about the countryside. He continued to write poetry, professing his love for his country and his people, but the dishonor of an unwarranted exile became a burden to his soul. He was further shattered when he learned of Chu's eventual fall to its rival, the state of Qin.

So, on the fifth day of the fifth lunar month in approximately 278 BC, Qu Yuan, with his arms clasped firmly around a huge rock, walked down to the Miluo River and threw himself into its torrents. According to legend, it was on the shore of the Miluo that Qu Yuan composed one of his most beautiful poems – a summary of his life and a farewell to the world. The poem, a lament known as the *Li-Sao (Encountering Sorrow)*, was Qu Yuan's longest and a masterpiece of pre-Han verse. The following excerpt, translated by David Hawkes in *Ch'u Tz'u: The Songs of the South*, poignantly captures the poem's deep anguish and provides an interesting allusion to the mythological beast that would one day become inextricably linked with the poet:

> Many a heavy sigh I heaved in my despair,
> Grieving that I was born in such an unlucky time,
> I plucked soft lotus petals to wipe my welling tears
> That fell down in rivers and wet my coat front.
> I knelt on my outspread skirts and poured my plaint out,

DRAGON BOATS: A CELEBRATION

And the righteousness within me was clearly manifest.
I yoked a team of jade dragons to a phoenix-figured car
And waited for the wind to come, to soar up on my journey.

News of Qu Yuan's suicide spread quickly among the villagers. Hundreds of local fishermen raced out in their boats in an attempt to save him, but to no avail. They beat their drums and splashed their paddles in the water to prevent fish and water dragons from eating his body. To ensure that his spirit would never waste away from hunger, the men scattered rice on the water.

According to legend, in 40 BC, the ghost of Qu Yuan appeared before the local fishermen. He explained to the men that his spirit was hungry because a river dragon had been eating the rice that was meant for him. To ward off the dragon so that his spirit could rest, he asked that the rice be wrapped in silk and tied with the colors of the emperor – in threads of red, blue, white, yellow, and black. These were colors also known to be dreaded by the water dragon.

Records reveal that such rice packets were first used by the peasantry during the Jin dynasty (266–316 AD) to celebrate the summer solstice. To this day these pyramid-shaped rice dumplings, or *zong zi*, remain a specialty food and have become synonymous with the dragon boat festival. Bamboo stems or lien leaves have replaced the silk jackets, and string has been substituted for the five-colored threads, while different kinds of knots are used to bind the filling and serve to indicate what is inside.

Opposite: Rotating dragon head at Nanhu Stadium, overlooking the race site at Yueyang.

Below: In a timeless reenactment of the search for Qu Yuan's body, residents of Yueyang reinvoke the spirit of China's great poet-statesman.

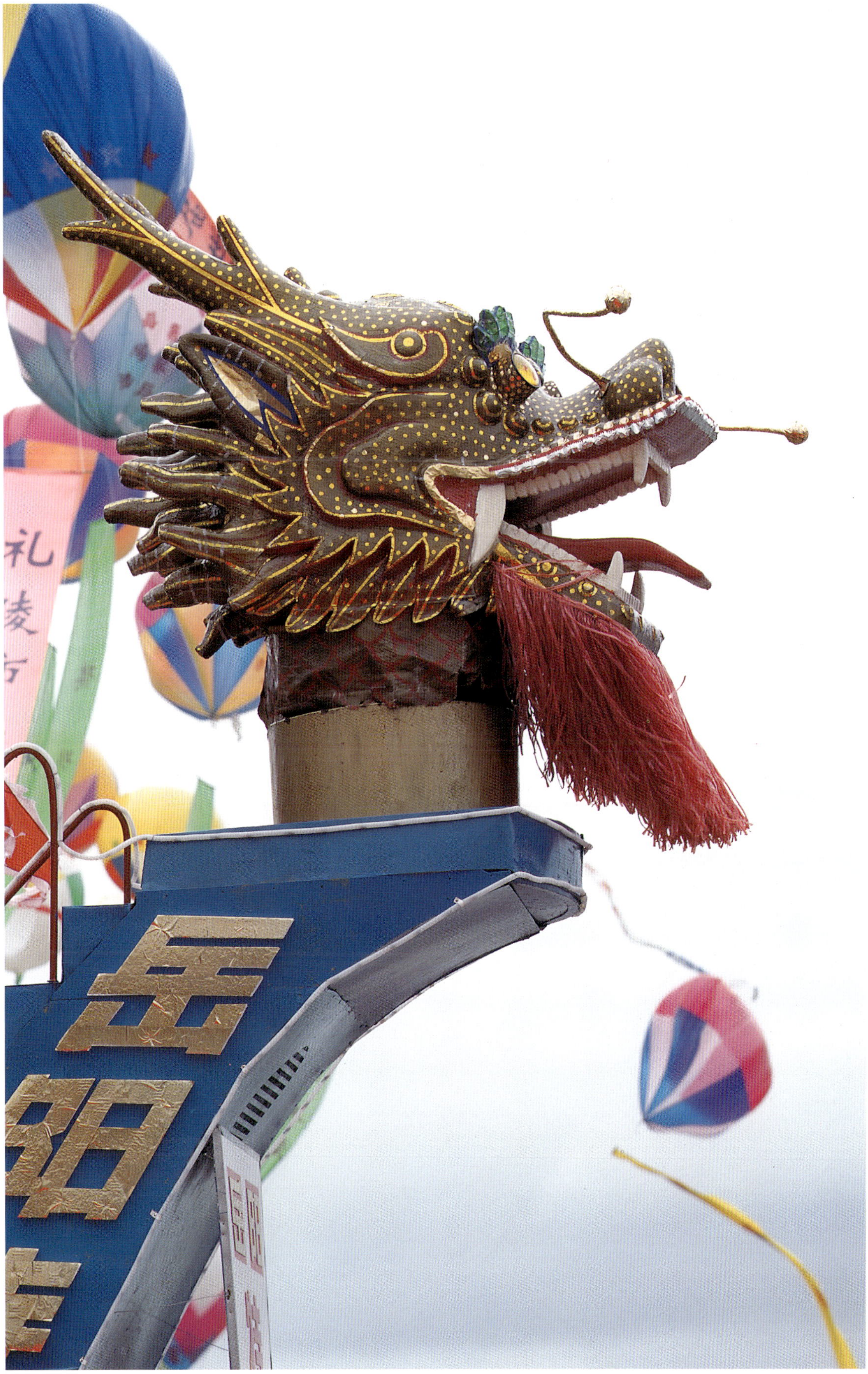

DRAGON BOATS: A CELEBRATION

A variety of combinations are made from three staple fillings: meat, bean, and lye. Yellowish-green and smaller, lye *zong zi* are preserved in a strong caustic alkaline solution known as *jian shui* and combined with a bit of sapanwood to ward off evil. The more preserved the dumpling, folk wisdom dictated, the higher its potency. Dysentery sufferers, particularly, were thought to benefit from these old, hardened dumplings, especially when they were ground into juice or liquid from pomegranate flowers.

Each region specializes in its own uniquely flavored *zong zi*. Beijing's *zong zi* are made with a sweet filling of bean paste, as are the dumplings found in Guangdong Province. Fillings of walnut and dates are also popular in this region. In other areas of southern China a glutinous rice mixture is wrapped in rice, palm, or bamboo leaves, with salty fillings of meat, egg, roast duck, or chicken. Typically *zong zi* are four-sided, with pointed or rounded ends, but they can also be shaped into cones or cylinders.

The dragon boat race itself may have existed during the early Han dynasty (202 BC–220 AD), but there are no definitive records that it did. However, a late Han historian named Ying Shao, writing in the second century AD, observed in a commentary on the dragon boat festival that the celebration owed its existence to Qu Yuan.

The reason for the death of Qu Yuan remains obscure, but his memory lives on in the Duan Yang (High Noon) Festival that is cele-

Offerings to the goddess of the sea – the blessing ceremony at the Canadian International Dragon Boat Festival in Vancouver.

6

brated throughout China every year on the fifth day of the fifth lunar month, which occurs some time between the end of May and the end of June. Often called the Wu Yue Jie, or Festival of the Double Fifth, the Duan Yang probably staged dragon boat races to secure bountiful crops, thus making it one of the world's many fertility festivals.

The notion of a dying god is central to many ancient festivals and was often symbolized by some form of human sacrifice. Early dragon boat races involved great drama, with capsizing boats and violent fights that always ended in death. Whether this was coincidental or a planned sacrifice to the gods is difficult to prove. However, it seems that human sacrifice was an important element of the festival. Someone always had to die.

The death of Qu Yuan was a voluntary act, yet suicide is often used to screen the age-old custom of human sacrifice. In ancient China people who drowned or committed suicide by drowning often became cult figures. Regarded as powerful deities, they controlled the waters and were capable of sending beneficial rains or destructive floods. Chinese folklore tells of many such legends, all of which centered around human reparation, usually in the form of death by drowning. It has been recorded that in some regions of China a beautiful woman was chosen as the victim. Dressed in a wedding gown, she was sent down the rapids as a sacrifice to the gods.

In Guangzhou there is the story of Jin-hua fu-ren, a goddess who

Priests of the Ching Chung Daoist Church of Canada performing the blessing ceremony at Vancouver's dragon boat festival.

drowned during the Festival of the Double Fifth. She became a kind of protector of the festival and her fragrance magically filled the air. South of Shanghai there is a similar tale of a young woman who committed suicide upon learning of the death of her father, who drowned during the festival. Her body was supposedly found days later in the river, in perfect condition, and smelling of the most unusual, beautiful fragrance. It has also been recorded that during times of floods townspeople would offer a sacrifice, usually a child, to a gap in one of the walls that protected the banks of their local river.

During the Warring States period, there existed cultural groups who adopted the elegies of Qu Yuan and used them as sacrificial texts at festivals. The Dai people of southern China were one such group. They believed that the gods required a human sacrifice to ensure fertile crops. The Dai celebrated spring and summer in connection with the harvest of rice, which was a vital staple for them. They also believed that fertility was life – in plants, in animals, and in humans. Since humans were the strongest of the three, the sacrifice of a human being was believed to be the best offering. The Dai were notorious for their acts of human sacrifice, and a victim, usually a stranger, was offered to the gods in exchange for fertile fields.

Chinese settlers were often the unfortunate victims; in particular, scholars were in the most danger. These individuals took great pride in wearing beards which, to the Dai, were a sign of strength and fertility. The scholars would be ambushed, usually while traveling through the mountains, and held captive at a Dai village. There they would be treated like royalty – all the food they could eat and a choice of women to ensure that their fertility did not wane.

There are stories of ill-fated love affairs between these native women and the scholars and, on occasion, the two managed to escape and live out their lives in the mountains. More often, however, the scholars were sacrificed, with their bodies cut up and distributed in equal portions to the members of the village. Later, body parts were embedded in rice fields to ensure a prosperous harvest. Lucky was the villager who obtained the bearded head of the body, for he would be assured a bountiful season. The Dai were able to celebrate the death of a stranger without any feelings of guilt because they believed that the victim was sent to them from their gods. Thus, according to these tribesmen, they were merely fulfilling destiny for that person.

With the influence of Chinese civilization, however, such rituals were replaced by staged fights or wading contests between two different villages. Villagers on opposite sides of a narrow river would throw stones at one another until someone was killed. Occasionally

Originally built during the Han dynasty, the Quzi Temple near the Miluo River is one of the many shrines commemorating Qu Yuan.

the event turned into a wading contest across the river, often resulting in death. The victorious team would celebrate the victory with a sexual orgy. It is believed that this was actually the prelude to the dragon boat festival and that boats were only added later.

The moving force behind the Chinese dragon boat festival, and the principal reason that it has endured for thousands of years, is the Chinese people's belief in the celebration's ability to produce the lifegiving rain that guarantees good harvests. In fact, the Festival of the Double Fifth is the second most important festival after the Chinese lunar New Year. Records between the world wars show that every village in southern China that was located near a stream or other body of water owned a dragon boat.

Another explanation for the dragon boat festival is the ceremonial "ancestral visits" associated with the transplanting of rice. Taken from small fields, rice was transplanted or "drowned" in large, flooded fields. Afterward, a planting crew would call up the spirits of dead forebears to come to their boats and act as guardian deities, as well as to restore power and virility to the transplanted seeds of rice. Such a ritual was

Carved wooden dragon from Java, circa 1950. Dragon Tales Collection. Courtesy of the Canadian International Dragon Boat Festival and curator Sam Carter.

said to call back the *hun,* or spirit, of the rice, a common ceremony in China. *Chao hun* was a term used to describe a person whose *hun* was thought to wander over foreign lands. One method used to recall a dead person's *hun* was to climb onto a roof and wave an article of the dead person's clothing while crying out loudly to the deceased's soul. A festival would be held to commemorate this important occasion, and dragon boats would be raced out in the direction of the newly transplanted fields. These races were thought to influence the growth of the rice and wash away bad tidings with the departure of dead souls.

After the poet Qu Yuan's suicide, many Chinese attempted to recall his *hun* in a similar manner, and the dragon boat festival was said to have originated with the ongoing search for the great man's spirit. An ancient Chinese dragon boat song expresses this sentiment hauntingly:

> Qu Yuan, where are you?
> If he is there, let us return.
> If he is not there, let us return.
> Do not linger on the riverbank.
> The cold wind is blowing.

Dragon boats were traditionally raced from north, the region of death, to south, the realm of life. When a boat passed through the finish line to victory, it was paddled backward while the racers took turns beating gongs and holding their paddles upright. The purpose of this ritual was to get in touch with the wandering *hun* of the rice and escort it back to the fields.

Dragon boat depicted on an ancient bronze drum from Vietnam.

However, dragon boats were not only used for ceremonial functions. Pirates and water police used canoes resembling dragon boats in the 19th century. Nor were such boats limited to the southern Chinese; records show that similar craft were used in Cambodia and Vietnam in the third century AD.

While boats used in northern Hunan Province were traditionally 75 to 115 feet long and carried 40 to 80 people, vessels found in Fuzhou and other areas of southern China were not as long and usually held crews of 28 to 36, making them closer in size and capacity to modern dragon boats. According to local sources in Yueyang in Hunan, there still exists a boat that can carry up to 300 people. The boats of ancient Cambodia and Vietnam were similar in size to those of Hunan, measuring 70 to 80 feet in length and carrying as many as 100 people.

These long vessels were capable of great speeds, but their considerable length made them particularly fragile in the middle. As a result, they often "hogged" or cracked in half. To prevent such mishaps, braided bamboo ropes, or hogging trusses, were placed around the gunwales and under the overhang at bow and stern, thus ensuring that a long boat would not break up.

The motif of the dragon on the bow and stern of Cambodian long boats was eventually replaced by that of a fish head and tail. It is possible that boats similar to these and the dragon boat were used in voyages involving vast distances on the open sea. Early European visitors to Thailand speak of substantial craft that were dug out of entire tree trunks and were elevated at the ends. Extra freeboard was added by tying planks along the gunwales. Records indicate that these boats were as much as 100 feet long and carried a crowd of 100. The Siamese royal barge, 150 feet long and 11 feet wide, was of similar construction. Comparable craft have been documented from Laos. These boats were painted black and gold, with red lacquer interiors. Besides the dragon, countries such as Vietnam, Cambodia, and Laos decorated their boats with other animals, usually those that were water-dwellers.

The so-called "many-handed" boat of Kumano, Japan, is still used in special ceremonies. The Japanese were thought to have added sails to the boat in later periods. Natives of the Ryukyu archipelago – a chain of islands off the coast of Japan extending southwest to Taiwan – also used dragon boats in ritual ceremonies, while Indonesia has stories of dragon boats that were communally owned. Similarly each village in Borneo had at least one long, communally owned war canoe. The Borneans, too, used planks stitched onto the gunwales to add extra freeboard. Chiefs or other well-respected men of distinction would sit under shelters made of large palm leaves to protect themselves from the hot sun. Heads on these boats were that of dogs or crocodiles, usually painted black and red.

Ranging in length from 70 to more than 100 feet, these boats were propelled by crews of 70 men armed with three-foot-long paddles. In this particular type of boat both the bow paddler and two stern paddlers were responsible for steering the boat, which was quite a different steering method than that of the Chinese and their more sophisticated steering oar. Also unlike the Chinese boats, which were known for their instability, the dugout canoes from Borneo were quite seaworthy and could venture out into open sea. It is believed that it was originally just such craft that the Kayan people used to reach Borneo.

Boat racing was also widespread in Southeast Asia, and there are records of such races occurring in Java, Japan, Thailand, and Burma. In China dragon boat races were traditionally celebrated in the regions that had most recently been assimilated by the expanding Chinese culture group pressing down from the north. The eminent Chinese

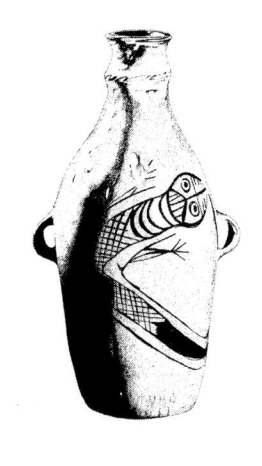

Painted pottery vase of China's Neolithic Yangshao culture (4000-2400 BC).

*Rubber dragon boat from
Borneo, 1992. Courtesy of the Sam Carter Collection.*

book, the *Yü Kung,* which is believed to date back to the first millennium BC, states that northern China was noted for its luxuriant vegetation and great trees. Similar trees were noted in southern and central China and were undoubtedly hollowed into the ancestral forms of present-day Chinese dragon boats.

Obviously dragon boats and the customs and rituals that surround them have very ancient origins. And as with anything else of such antiquity, one can find ample evidence of long-ago practices in modern activities. One of the most colorful rituals surrounding today's dragon boat festival is the traditional "awakening" of the dragons. Although the ceremonial side of the festival is less well-known than the athletic side, this ancient ceremony has a deep cultural heritage rooted in religious beliefs. The procedure for blessing the boats varies in detail from one festival to another, but each blessing conveys a deep reverence for the vessel. The ceremony in Vancouver, British Columbia, is performed by a Daoist priest, who is invited by festival organizers.

Daoism, which originated in China, is one of the oldest religions in the world. In its essence it represents certain principles: the spirit of harmony with nature, balance and loyalty, honor and devotion, freedom and compassion for all, selfless service, and action through nonaction. It is believed that by acting in accordance with these principles an individual will be brought closer to the truth of reality.

In Hunan Province dragon boats are stored in long, low sheds against the village temple. In the fourth lunar month a committee is sent from the temple to call upon the people for a regular contribution. Often this task is carried out by boat women who carry bamboo trays for the collections and a flag representing their temple.

Four days prior to the festival the dragon boats are taken out of storage and the heads and tails are attached. Ceremonial chanting then begins, which is thought to invoke the Daoist saints and immortals to ward off evil while blessing and cleansing the race site. The chants are also thought to appease spirits that might impede victory, and in a similar fashion offerings such as food and wine are made to the dragon boats themselves. Often an exorcist performs somersaults from prow to stern, then scatters buckwheat and purifies the boat with fire while drums scare away any lingering evil.

Next, paper bills *(fu zhou),* incense, or candles are burned in front of the boats as an offering to the goddess of the sea. On race day the priest may light oil in front of the dragon boat. Flames that reach high in the sky forecast victory for this particular boat, while a dim flame predicts defeat. Such bad omens can be countered with the use of powerful spells such as the one found at the beginning of this chapter. When all such spells have been uttered, the priest brushes off any further evil influences with wisps of grass.

Dragon boats are awakened, or given life, during the traditional Dotting of the Eye ceremony. Bright, colorful headpieces adorned with peacock feathers are placed on the dragon's head, and vermilion paint, mixed with the blood of a brown chicken, is dabbed on the dragon's forehead for courage. The priest then rings a bell with one hand, while using the other hand to stab a *fu zhou* with his sword. The *fu zhou* is inscribed with magic words that are chanted by the priest while he blesses the head, the tail, and the drum with the sword. An invited guest of the community is given the honor of dotting the eyes with red paint to give the dragon sight. Finally a handful of buckwheat is thrown into the boat to give it speed and good luck. The boats are now ready for the approaching races.

Just as there are rituals to awaken the boats, so are there rituals to put them back to sleep. After the races, when the festival is over, the head, tail, and drum are removed from the boats. Then, with flags rolled up, the boats are paddled in silence and stored in either a temple or a place agreed upon by the community. The body of the boat is traditionally covered with sand or stored on racks that are covered with tinfoil in the shape of roofs. In return for their hard work and commitment to the dragon boat festival, some communities believe they will be rewarded with a prosperous year and will be protected

These dancers from China are an example of one of the many cultural events that take place at Vancouver's Canadian International Dragon Boat Festival.

Blessing ceremony altar dedicated to the goddess of the sea, the saints, and the immortals. In traditional Chinese practice five offerings, representing the five elements, are made to the five directions.

from unwelcome water spirits.

Repairs and fresh paint are applied to the dragon boats the following year, and once more the cycle begins with the Awakening of the Dragon ceremony. Most appropriately, in Hunan Province, an offering is made and an exorcist recites an ancient Chinese spell over the boats: "As the dark waters down the river flow, so may all maladies, diseases, plagues, and death go."

Hosting dragon boat races is thought to bring health, happiness, and prosperity, as well as offer protection from the unfriendly spirits of the sea. In cities around the world as diverse as Vancouver, Berlin, Singapore, Sydney, and New York, much of the ceremonial aspect of dragon boat racing is maintained, and it is not hard to imagine that many of the thousands who flock to witness this ancient sport come away with a renewed appreciation for life.

Community dignitaries assist with the Dotting of the Eye ceremony to awaken the spirit of the dragon at Vancouver's dragon boat festival.

Dragons Through the Ages

Of all the world's mythical creatures, few are more celebrated or as ancient as the dragon. The first recorded dragon myth (circa 2000 BC) is that of the slaying of Tiamat, the Babylonian mother goddess dragon killed by one of her progeny, Marduk, king of the gods. Many scholars believe that this myth, part of the Mesopotamian creation story and assembled from elements of Egyptian mythology, served as the catalyst for the development of similar myths throughout the world. However, recent discoveries of Chinese utensils bearing carvings of dragons, unearthed in Henan Province, China, have proven that the notion of this mythological beast dates back 6,000 years in the Far East.

In Babylonian mythology Tiamat represented darkness, chaos, and the destructive side of human nature. Vestiges of the story of her slaying can be found in later European and Near Eastern myths in which heroes such as Michael the Archangel, the biblical Daniel, Perseus, Hercules, Siegfried, Beowulf, and St. George vanquish some form of monstrous dragon. Although there is a dark side to the dragon in Chinese mythology, often portrayed as two opposing dragons embodying the concept of yin and yang, people in the Far East view the dragon as a largely positive, beneficial entity. Where Western heroes and gods always seek to annihilate evil, Chinese philosophy and myth speak of balancing and harmonizing eternal opposites.

Mythographers speculate that the dragon originated as a totem along with wind, fire, rain, and clouds. The Chinese believed that they were directly related to dragons and that they would be transformed into these mythical creatures when they died. Dragons found on pottery and other artifacts of the Yangshao (4000–2400 BC) and Longshan (2400–2200 BC) cultures had either the head of a human or an animal, the body of a snake or a fish, and were covered with fins or the mane of a horse. Scales began to appear on the dragon by the time of the legendary Xia dynasty (2200–1766 BC), and the motif was used extensively on jadeware and bronzes of the Shang dynasty (1766–1122 BC). Carvings found on Shang tortoiseshells indicate that the dragon had also been associated with praying for rain and agricultural production at least a thousand or more years before the death of Qu Yuan and the possible origins of the dragon boat festival. By the Zhou dynasty (1122–256 BC), horns had been added to the dragon image as well as pointed fins along its back.

During the Warring States period (481–221 BC), literary and artistic depictions of the dragon became

Beijing opera coat, 1990. Courtesy of the Sam Carter Collection.

more detailed and animated. By the time of the Han dynasty (202 BC–220 AD), the dragon image began to appear on murals, silk clothing, and tombs. Similarly the Shu kingdom (221–263 AD) employed the dragon image on eaves tiles to decorate palace buildings. The tiles had four different designs that were based on Chinese mythology and the four points of the compass. North was represented by the tortoise, south by the rosefinch, west by the white tiger, and east by the black dragon. It was during the Han dynasty, however, that the dragon took on a more consistent appearance. Han dragons were depicted with a python's body, a tiger's feet, a bearded head, and the tail of a fish.

With the introduction of Buddhism to China in the fourth and fifth centuries AD, there was an assimilation of the *naga* of Indian myth with the dragon of Chinese folklore. The *naga* had no feet and a long, snakelike body. Its name means "dragon," and it was known as the leader of the snakes. There were four *nagas;* each had great powers and ruled over the four seas that surrounded the Earth. According to legend, Buddha was invited by a dragon to visit his crystal palace at the bottom of the sea. A new folklore thus arose during this period, one that included dragons in the "four seas" as well as dragon kings that ruled rivers, lakes, and streams.

The Chinese believe in four principal types of dragons. First, there are the celestial fire-breathers, or *long*, which are considered to be the most powerful and were identified with the Chinese emperor. These five-clawed creatures live high in the clouds, have infinite supernatural powers, and are thought to be the vital essence. It is said that these dragons cannot hear, which is why the hearing-impaired in China are also called *long*. The second type of dragon, known as *li,* live in the sea. These hornless dragons breathe foam and water and have the ability to make rain. They also rule over the four points of the compass. *Mang,* the third type of dragon, has four claws and is viewed as the common dragon that holds sway over temporal power. The last dragon, *jiao*, lives in the earth under hills that it created for itself with its back. This dragon's breath is still believed to bring good fortune. It is revered by those who follow *feng shui,* a body of principles that has been practiced since the Tang dynasty (618–907 AD). *Feng shui,* which literally means "wind and water," is the ability to "harness the dragon's breath" in order to bring happiness, prosperity, and good health.

Today the *long* is considered the authentic dragon image and is the most worshipped. Its head is to the south and its tail to the north. According to the Daoists, this dragon has nine likenesses, which are usually portrayed in a number of ways. To some it has the head of a camel, the ears of a cow, the neck of a snake, and the belly of a frog. Its horns have been taken from the deer and its scales from the fish. The eyes of the *long* come from the rabbit and its feet from both the claws of the hawk and the palm of the tiger. This practice of dissecting various animals and then reshaping them in the form of a new one is a common feature of Chinese art. Nothing is ever discarded. Everything is used to create new forms.

By the time of the Sui (581–618 AD) and Tang dynasties, standards for the depiction of the dragon image were further developed. Eventually a group known as the Fish and Dragon School was set up in the period of the Five dynasties (907–960 AD). During this time and in later years, greater emphasis was placed on achieving the nine likenesses of the dragon in painting.

The Mongol rulers of the Yuan dynasty (1264–1368 AD) prohibited the use of the dragon in painting because it had become the official emblem of the emperor. When the prohibition was ignored, the emperor decided to compromise with the people by allowing them to depict dragons with three claws. The five-clawed dragon remained solely for the emperor's use. This tradition continued into the Ming (1368–1644 AD) and Qing (1644–1912 AD) dynasties, which both claimed that an authentic dragon must have five claws; anything with fewer claws was considered a python.

The mythology and image of the dragon has permeated both Chinese and Western cultures. However, for the Chinese people the dragon's long history has had such a profound effect that it is associated with virtually every part of their lives. There are dragons that protect the home, dragons that exert restraint over gluttony and greed, and spiritual dragons that produce wind and rain. Today's competitive dragon boat racers may not view their contests as symbolic rain-producing clashes between heavenly dragons, but much of the excitement, intensity, and spectacle still prevail in a sport that continues to attract legions of fans in countries Qu Yuan could never have imagined.

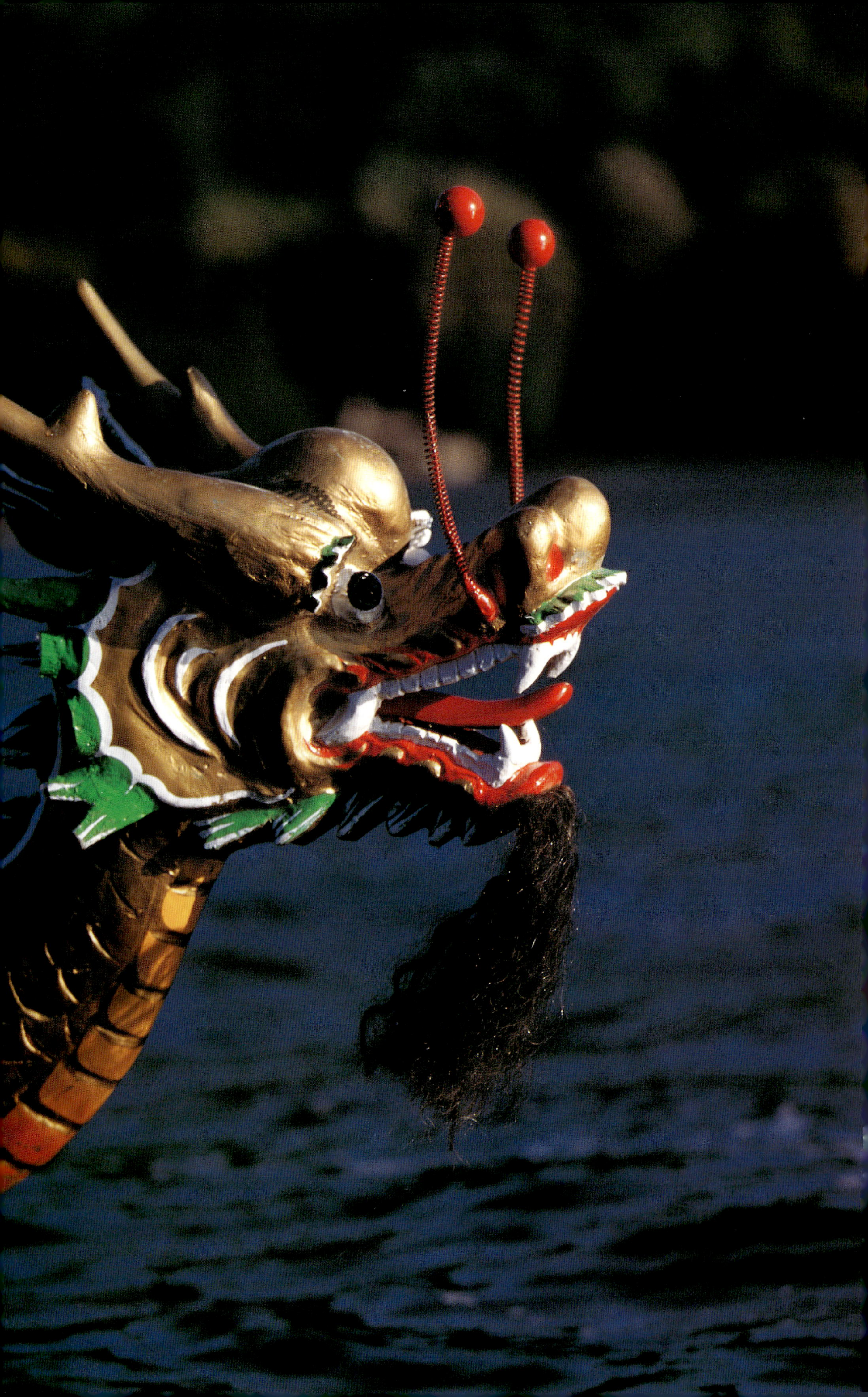

2 Shaping the Dragon

Boats and Builders

With bare hands the artisan hammers the sides of his fists into the blocks of wood. A few gentle hits on one piece, a few harder hits on another, back and forth until a flawless consonance has been achieved. "This piece is called the fan," says Vincent Lo, co-owner of Six-Sixteen Dragon Boats Limited. Then he gives the block of wood one last stroke, perhaps just for good luck. "The fan serves a purpose in the wooden dragon boat, but it is strictly decorative in the fiberglass boat," he explains.

What is firmly established cannot be uprooted.
What is firmly grasped cannot slip away.
It will be honored from generation to generation.

VINCENT, OR "VINNY," as he is known to his friends, has managed Vancouver's False Creek Women's Dragon Boat Team since 1989 and has been finishing dragon boats since 1990. He and Don Irvine, former coach of the False Creek women's team, created a partnership and founded a company out of a growing necessity.

In the early years of the Vancouver Festival, the Chinese Cultural Centre organized practices and races using what were then the only teak dragon boats in Canada. To train for the local event, teams were allotted a mere four practices prior to the festival. So, due to the limited access, teams that wanted more extensive, year-round training resorted to using voyageur canoes. These canoes, which can carry as many as 10 people, were not without their limitations, but at the time they were the best training tools available.

After four years of training in the voyageurs, Irvine and Lo realized that if the team wanted to compete at the highest international level, it was essential to train in a dragon boat. The sport's popularity was increasing at an incredible rate, and although the team had attained an unofficial world championship title, further improvement would be

The dragon is one of the world's most potent symbols. Here it is displayed in all its glory as the figurehead of a teak dragon boat in Hong Kong.

difficult without the ability to train in dragon boats year-round.

The two men contemplated using the teak dragon boat as a prototype, but in just four years of festival use these boats were already showing signs of wear. Teak may have the best properties for a marine application — stability, density, durability, high oil content — but the wood has certain peculiarities that Irvine and Lo had to consider. Dragon boats made of teak are not only expensive, but the availability of large teak planks is problematic. A further disadvantage with wood is that when it is alternately exposed to humid and dry conditions, it shrinks and expands, often resulting in boat leakage. In ancient China such leakage problems were solved by storing boats in sand, which kept them moist and prolonged their lives.

Irvine and Lo knew one of their greatest problems would be storage. Boats left in water would be exposed to sun, salt, and rain. Marine growth would shorten their life spans and add to their maintenance. However, due to the great length and weight of teak dragon boats, storing them on land would be far more difficult than storing lighter fiberglass boats.

Another consideration for the two builders was the provision of ample leg room and boat capacity for larger, heavier North American paddlers. The shorter, heavier teak boats offered less leg room between seats, something more suited to smaller, lighter Asian paddlers. In designing their own boat, Lo suggested that they include extra seats to allow spare racers in the boat for training sessions rather than leave them onshore.

Eventually their specifications for a new boat included four extra seats, increased leg room (by redesigning the bulkheads), and the use of fiberglass as a construction material. Half the weight of dry teak boats, fiberglass craft require less maintenance, are less likely to leak, and are remarkably comparable in weight when produced from the same mold. "We take great care in making sure the boats are very even in weight," says Irvine. "There isn't more than 30 pounds difference between each of our fiberglass boats." Teak boats, on the other hand, can vary in weight by as much as hundreds of pounds. Finally fiberglass boats can be stored in or out of the water with less worry about the kind of rot and deterioration that teak boats can suffer.

Irvine and Lo turned to a company in Hong Kong to make their initial mold, and in May 1990 two fiberglass boats were sent by ship to Vancouver. Special arrangements were required to ship the two dragon boats. Unlike the teak boats from Hong Kong whose dimensions were built with ship transport in mind, the fiberglass boats were at least eight feet longer than the 40-foot ship containers. As a result, the boats were carried on the ship's deck "for a rather substantial fee," reports Lo.

Arriving at Vancouver Terminal in Burrard Inlet on a blustery spring day, 40 False Creek Racing Canoe Club members paddled the two boats more than eight miles in chilly conditions to the False Creek Community Centre on Granville Island. In effect, this journey was the boats' first big test; if these longer craft could survive the rough waves of the unprotected harbor, they would meet the safety objectives of the designer. Cold and wet, the two crews arrived at Granville Island with unscathed boats. However, the performance objectives of the boats would still have to be proved.

After this daunting journey, one of the boats was sent off to a local fiberglass shop to serve as a prototype. Six-Sixteen Dragon Boats, whose name refers to the number of progressive strokes Vancouver dragon boat teams use to get a boat up and running (see page 60), was in business. The company sold its first six boats to the Vancouver Festival, which by this time had become known as the Canadian International Dragon Boat Festival. Today the festival operates a fleet of nine teak boats from Hong Kong and nine fiberglass boats built in Vancouver by Six-Sixteen.

FIBERGLASS, ALTHOUGH FIRST invented in the 19th century, was not used significantly in manufacturing until the Second World War stimulated a demand for new materials. Today the wondrous "fabric" that many 19th-century skeptics felt would never have much practical application is used to make everything from household curtains to automobile parts – and, of course, boats.

The first step in building a fiberglass dragon boat is to find a prototype from which to produce a mold. The surface of the prototype has to be as perfect and as smooth as possible. Dents are filled in and the boat is sanded until its finish is mirror-smooth. "Unless the mold is perfect," insists Vincent Lo, "any dragon boat you make from it will pick up every single flaw from the original."

A mold kept in immaculate condition can produce many dragon boats. To keep a mold in good shape, a dragon boat is left finished, or partially finished, in the mold until it is needed to make a new boat. This procedure protects the mold against dust, sharp objects, or anything that might fall into it and cause damage.

Making a fiberglass dragon boat takes approximately six weeks from start to finish. The fiberglass hull is usually completed in four weeks, then Lo, in his spare time, does the wood finishing over a two-week period.

The next step involves applying a release wax to the surface of the

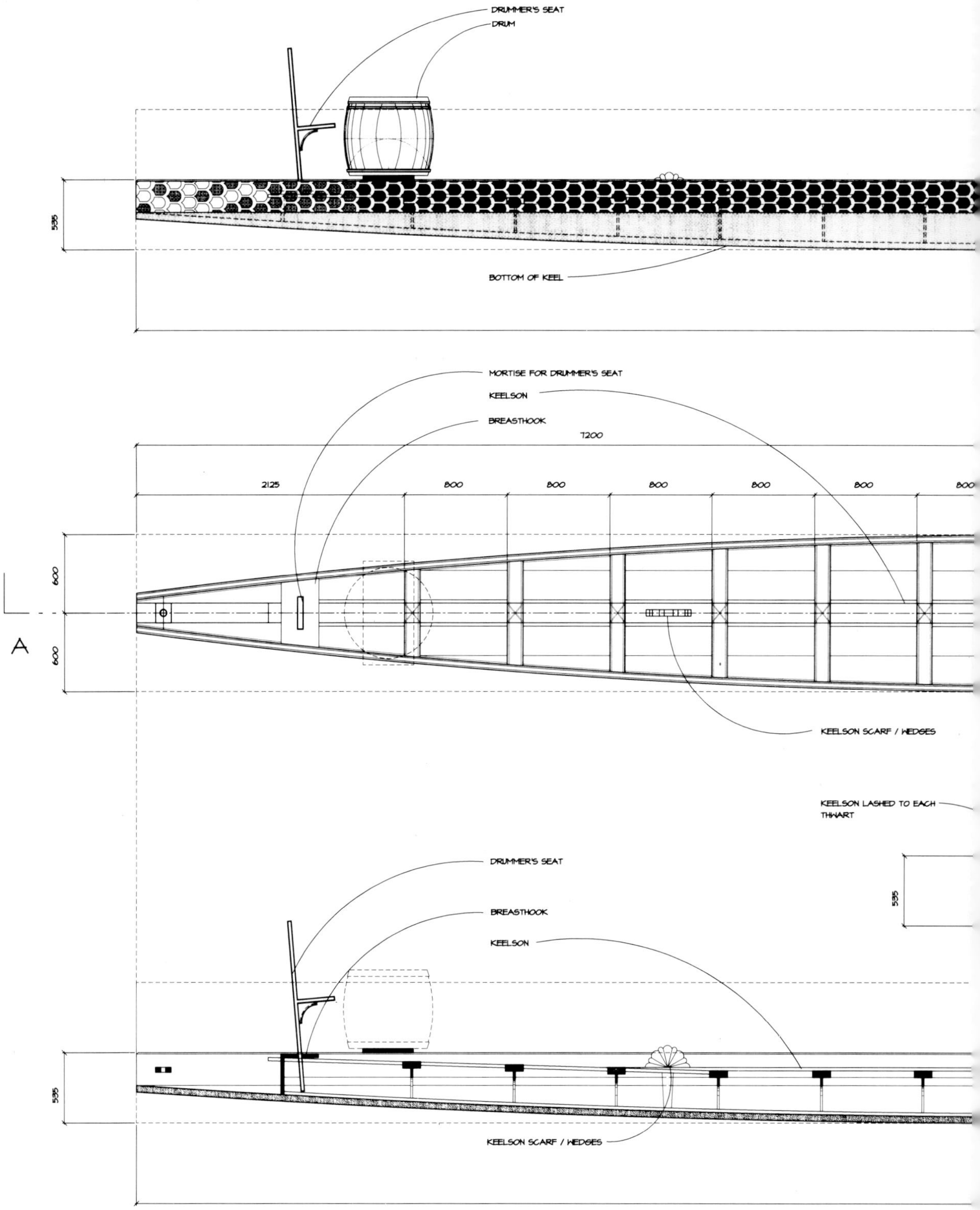

DRUMMER'S SEAT
DRUM
535
BOTTOM OF KEEL
MORTISE FOR DRUMMER'S SEAT
KEELSON
BREASTHOOK
7200
2125
800
800
800
800
800
800
600
600
A
KEELSON SCARF / WEDGES
KEELSON LASHED TO EACH THWART
535
DRUMMER'S SEAT
BREASTHOOK
KEELSON
535
KEELSON SCARF / WEDGES

Fiberglass Dragon Boat

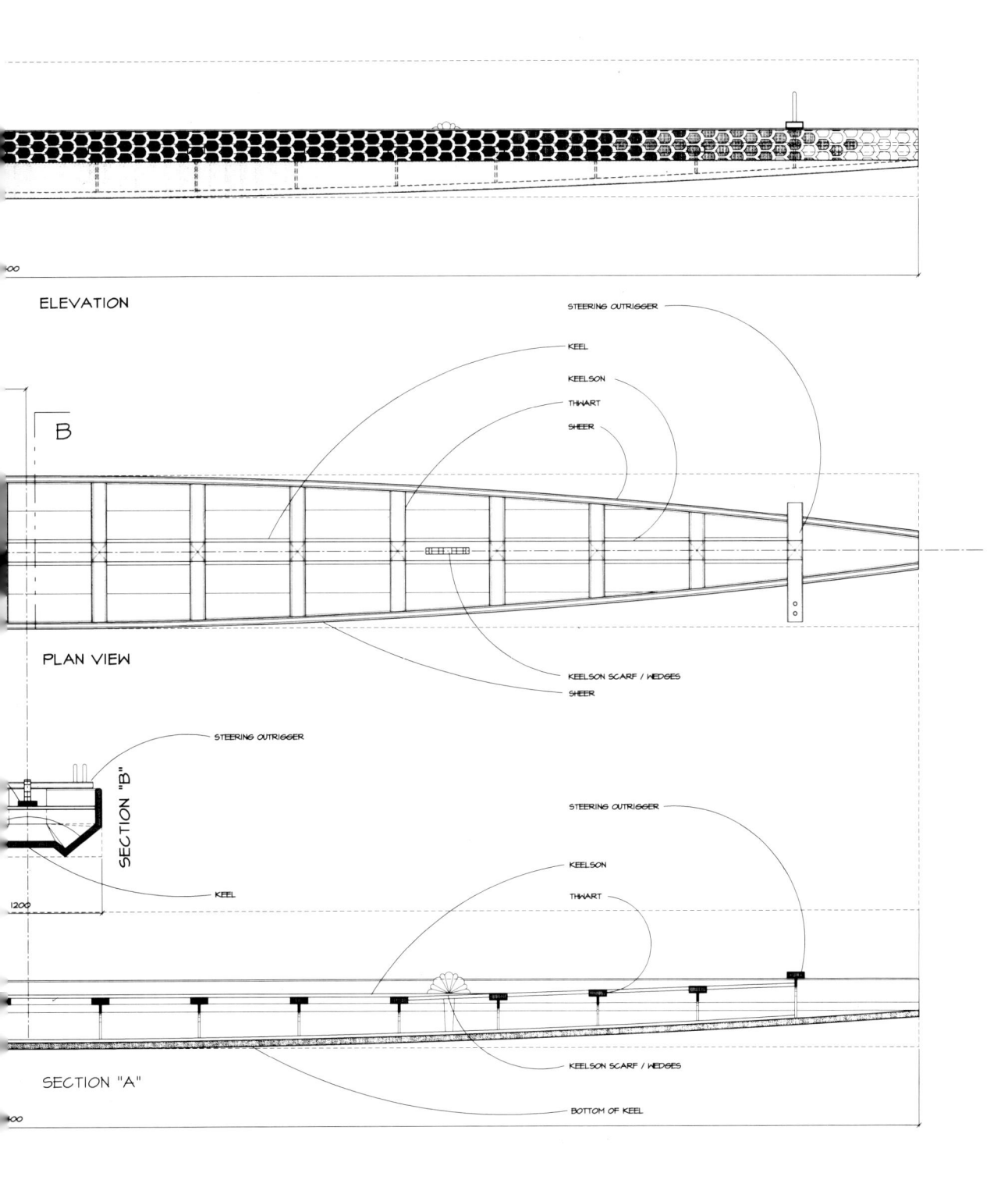

ELEVATION

STEERING OUTRIGGER
KEEL
KEELSON
THWART
SHEER

PLAN VIEW

KEELSON SCARF / WEDGES
SHEER

STEERING OUTRIGGER
KEEL

SECTION "B"

STEERING OUTRIGGER
KEELSON
THWART

KEELSON SCARF / WEDGES
BOTTOM OF KEEL

SECTION "A"

DRAGON BOATS: A CELEBRATION

Vincent Lo working resin into one of the many layers of matt. Courtesy Six-Sixteen Dragon Boats Limited.

mold, which prevents the boat's hull from becoming stuck in the mold. Fiberglass hulls are made of many distinct layers. The outermost layer, known as gel coat, is a special opaque resin that is scratch-resistant and waterproof and gives the final product its color and shiny finish. It is sprayed on evenly, usually in a hue that will contrast with the color of the mold, a practice that allows a builder to see what needs to be sprayed. Once this first layer is cured, it is then reinforced with numerous layers of fiberglass soaked in plastic resin. In effect, the fiberglass gives the boat its strength, while the resin holds the craft together.

The fiberglass layers of a dragon boat consist of numerous layers of matt and woven roving. Matt is composed of short-strand glass fibers

26

that randomly crisscross and interlock with one another. The fibers can be pulled apart because they consist of dried, unactivated fiberglass strands that are highly absorbent of the resin.

The woven products consist of long, continuous strands woven together like cloth. These strands are of varying thicknesses; the thinner the strand, the lighter the weight. The lightest weave is called "angel hair," a heavier weave is known as "cloth," and the heaviest weave is named "roving." Woven roving is similar in appearance to a woven basket in that heavy bundles of fibers are woven at right angles to one another. The space between these woven fibers, or bundles, permits the resin to flow and wet the glass fibers.

Seven different seat molds are used in building a fiberglass hull: two seats per mold, or 14 in total. Each seat is glassed in place at three anchor points and is a little longer and taller than the next seat. While teak boats gain their rigidity from the bulkhead and keelson (center railing), fiberglass boats are provided with stiffness by their seats and keelson.

Closed-cell foam is inserted in the fiberglass seat cavities to provide floatation capability if the boat takes on water. The foam consists of tiny air cells that don't connect with one another, thus preventing waterlogging. Like fiberglass, this material was developed during World War II for a wide variety of uses, particularly in the floatation of navy boats and docks. Since closed-cell foam neither rusts nor corrodes, it is practically maintenance-free except for a tendency to discolor.

Next, the fiberglass-molded seats are topped with Douglas fir from British Columbia. According to Vincent Lo, this type of wood was chosen because of its light weight, strength, and reasonable price. Douglas fir is also used in the drummer's seat, keelson, and fan, while western maple, eastern red oak, and mahogany are used in other areas of the boats either for their specific abilities or their visual appeal. Two screws are drilled through the keelson into each seat to hold it in place, and screw holes are filled with wooden plugs.

The keel, which was copied from the one found in teak dragon boats, is seven inches wide by three-quarters of an inch thick. However, unlike teak, which can twist or buckle, says Irvine, "the inert properties of fiberglass make it impossible for boats made from it to buckle."

Nine feet longer than the teak dragon boat, the 48-foot fiberglass craft gains another five feet with the addition of its head and tail. These bow and stern adornments are by far the most unique and decorative features of the dragon boat. A two-piece mold is used to create the tail, but the head has a more elaborate 11-part construction: a single piece for

DRAGON BOATS: A CELEBRATION

Vancouver artist Anne-Marie Nehring invests each dragon boat with a unique personality.

the dragon's tongue, four pieces for the upper and lower jaw and face, two pieces for the body, two pieces for the dragon's horns, and two pieces for the section that holds the dragon's whiskers. When fully assembled, the head and tail are sent to Vancouver artist Anne-Marie Nehring, who also happens to be the steersperson for the False Creek women's team. Nehring brings the pieces to life with her own personal flair, using a spectrum of hot pinks and neon-greens complemented by the more traditional Chinese red and gold. Vinyl scales are applied to the sides of the boat, and by the time Nehring has finished painting, each head-and-tail assembly will invest its respective boat with a unique personality.

After they have been painted, the head and tail are placed in stainless-steel brackets that are loosely mounted onto the dragon boat. Lo's reason for this practice is that the boats are frequently paddled by inexperienced crews. Should a crew happen to collide with another boat or hit some other obstacle while docking, the head or tail will simply be knocked off and fall into the water where rescue will be relatively easy and damage kept at a minimum.

SHAPING THE DRAGON

WHILE FIBERGLASS BOATS may be superior to traditional teak craft in terms of speed and durability, there are those who believe nothing can compare to the feel and solidity of paddling a wooden boat. As mentioned already, teak dragon boats used in today's international races measure nearly 39 feet, with the head-and-tail assembly increasing the overall length by four to seven feet. However, in China and Hong Kong teak boats are still made in a variety of lengths.

The Chinese refer to the smaller 39-foot craft as "canoes," while only the 50- to 60-foot "long" boats are called dragon boats. These longer, traditional vessels were fashioned for use on rivers, not as oceangoing craft. In addition, the boats were built so that they could be paddled forward or backward. This ability was crucial to the boats' ceremonial function in the return of the spirit of the rice, or *hun,* to transplanted fields during the Festival of the Double Fifth. It is also likely that the boats needed this capability since the races were usually held on narrow rivers with very little room for maneuvering. Such a design feature meant that paddlers merely had to turn themselves around at one end of the course and paddle back to the other end.

There are only a handful of teak dragon boat builders in Hong

Four drummer seats ready for shipment.

Kong today, and it takes four of these craftsmen two weeks to complete a boat. In recent years there has been a revival of this ancient Chinese art, and some craftsmen follow traditional methods of building boats by hand and eye, forsaking blueprints and modern equipment. However, even with today's tools, the construction of this ancient watercraft still requires great skill and dexterity.

Laying the keel is the first step in building a teak dragon boat. Like a human spine, the keel supports the body of the boat and must be straight in one plane and curved in the other. This is an important procedure that requires great care, for if the keel is built with no curve in the wrong plane (i.e., no rocker, thus flat), water will enter the boat during paddling. Likewise, if by mistake the straight plane is built in a curve, the boat will move in circles, or if the curved plane is accidentally made straight, the boat will sink.

The next step, and the most challenging, is the process of attaching the keel to other specially prepared planks of wood. Known as the *xiapang* and *dapang,* or small and big side, these pieces together form the "double-chined" bottom of the boat, enhancing the craft's overall stability. The curved rocker at either end makes the boat easier to maneuver.

After that the topsides or "skin" of the boat are made. Builders call these sections the *huapang* or decorative shell. When the hull is completed, special artisans are brought in to draw and paint the exquisite scales that cover it. Later, the seats and keelson, or *long-gen* (literally the "dragon root," as it is known in Hong Kong), are fitted into the boat. The keelson is a longitudinal member that runs the length of the boat across the top of the thwarts, to which it is lashed. Boats in the past were lashed with the tendons of animals; today a specially coated nylon rope, not unlike the ancient lashings in appearance, is used.

Composed of two pieces, the keelson is scarfed together between thwarts seven and eight with five wedges of wood known as the "fan." Unlike the two fans found in the fiberglass boat, whose purpose is purely decorative, the fans in the teak boat are attached to a support structure that prevents the vessel from buckling in the middle. The strength and stiffness the keelson adds to the teak hull's framework is best demonstrated at the dragon boat races in Hong Kong. Capsized boats weighing more than five tons are emptied by a crane whose two lifting points are at the keelson.

Curiously the 39-foot dragon boat's design has been partly dictated by the need for convenient transport. Standard ship containers, at their longest, measure 40 feet, which means that all items placed in them must be at least six inches shorter. As such, the teak boat's fair-

SHAPING THE DRAGON

ings, or gills, are removable. These pieces are located at both ends of the craft and are used as housings for the dragon head and tail. The fact that they are removable may provide some minor protection to the head and tail pieces in the event of a collision on the water.

Extreme care is taken during every step of construction, but special attention is given to nail work. Iron and copper nails are driven one-quarter of an inch below the surface, then plugged with wood filler. No fasteners are visible anywhere, and nails are spaced evenly every two inches down the length of the boat. Obviously hammering must be done carefully, since a boat will leak if any of the nails are broken.

The drummer sits up front on a removable wooden seat that is fitted through a slot in the forward breasthook and rests against a small wedge at the bottom of the boat. The drum, which is also removable, is lashed to a small platform fixed to the vessel's gunwale, while in the rear of the boat a 20-foot wooden steering oar is kept in place by two thole pins that are outrigged onto a wooden block.

The entire body of the wooden dragon boat is made of teak imported from Thailand and Burma. Teak is expensive but is valued for its durability and strength. Most Hong Kong builders subcontract the carving of the dragon head and tail to artisans in China. These intricate pieces are carved by hand out of camphor wood.

Although teak boats look beautiful when new, keeping them that way requires a great deal of maintenance. With special care a well-made teak dragon boat should last more than 20 years. However, they

Outrigged thole pins for supporting the steering oar on a fiberglass dragon boat.

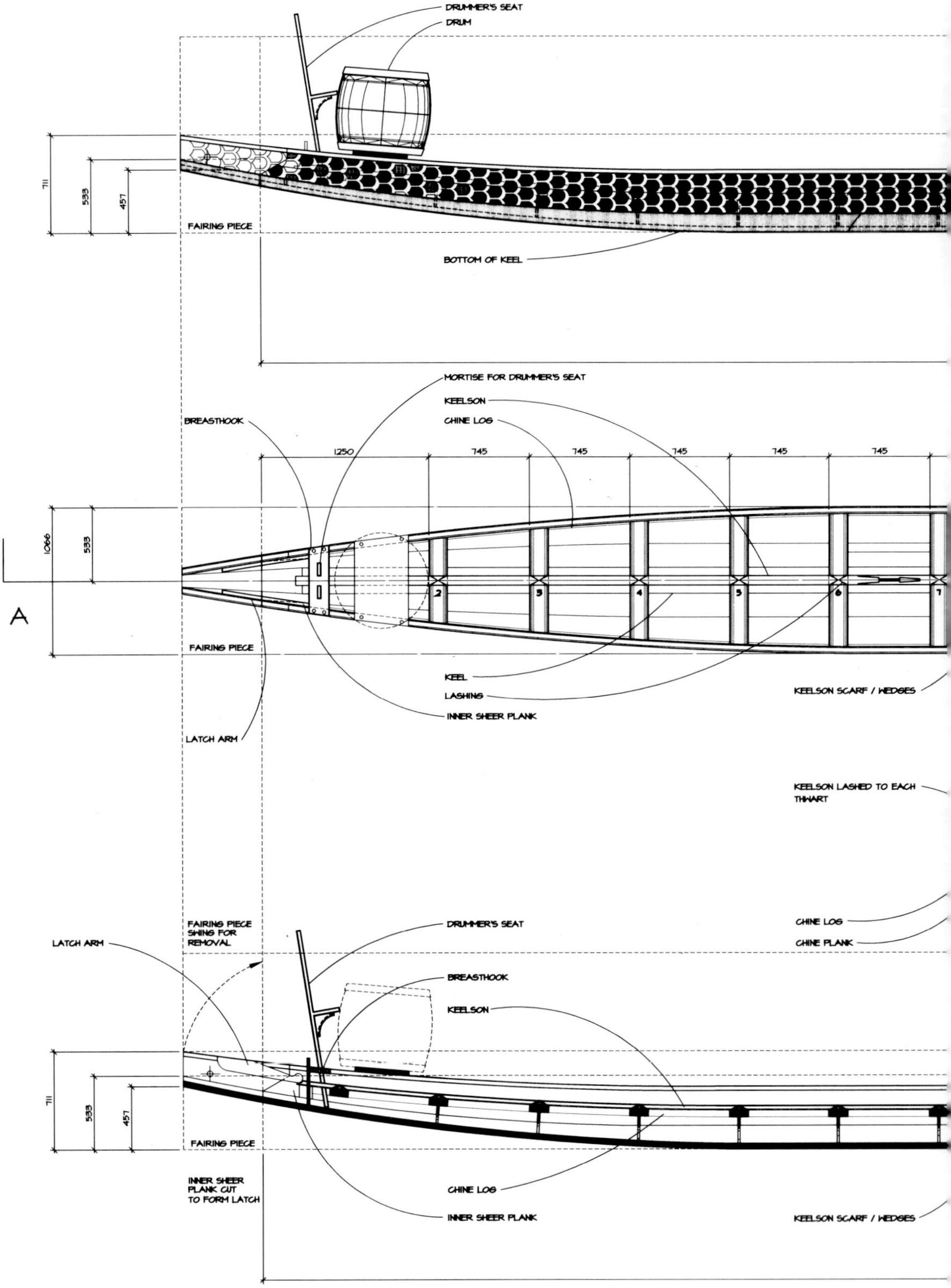

DRUMMER'S SEAT
DRUM
711
533
457
FAIRING PIECE
BOTTOM OF KEEL
MORTISE FOR DRUMMER'S SEAT
KEELSON
CHINE LOG
BREASTHOOK
1250
745
745
745
745
745
1066
533
A
2
3
4
5
6
7
FAIRING PIECE
KEEL
LASHING
INNER SHEER PLANK
KEELSON SCARF / WEDGES
LATCH ARM
KEELSON LASHED TO EACH THWART
CHINE LOG
CHINE PLANK
FAIRING PIECE SWING FOR REMOVAL
LATCH ARM
DRUMMER'S SEAT
BREASTHOOK
KEELSON
711
533
457
FAIRING PIECE
INNER SHEER PLANK CUT TO FORM LATCH
CHINE LOG
INNER SHEER PLANK
KEELSON SCARF / WEDGES

Teak Dragon Boat

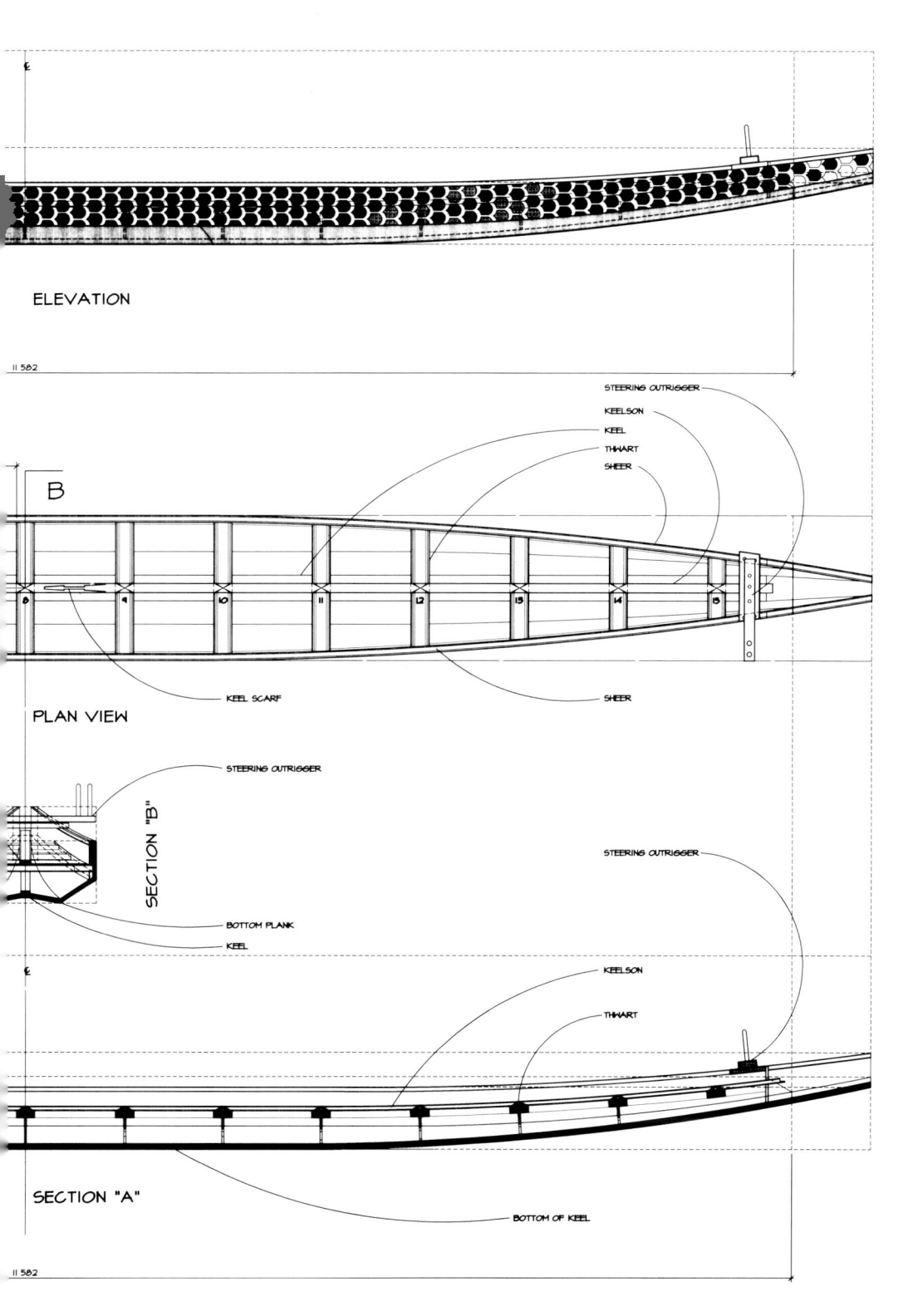

ELEVATION

PLAN VIEW

SECTION "B"

- STEERING OUTRIGGER
- KEELSON
- KEEL
- THWART
- SHEER
- KEEL SCARF
- SHEER
- STEERING OUTRIGGER
- BOTTOM PLANK
- KEEL

SECTION "A"

- STEERING OUTRIGGER
- KEELSON
- THWART
- BOTTOM OF KEEL

Vincent Lo applies the final touches to a new fiberglass dragon boat.

need to be repainted every year, which means the old coat of lacquer has to be removed so that the bare wood can be sanded smooth. Two new layers of lacquer are then applied to create a coating that will protect the boat from the elements.

The cost of a teak dragon boat varies from CDN $16,000 for the standard 39-foot boat to as much as CDN $30,000 for one of the larger dragon boats, which can carry up to 60 people. Fiberglass boats, on the other hand, can range in price from CDN $12,000 to $16,000, depending on how many accessories are added.

Six-Sixteen Dragon Boats Limited plans to introduce a new design to the North American market in the spring of 1996. These smaller "baby dragons" will be able to carry 10 paddlers and should prove to be an effective training tool, especially for smaller racing clubs. Having two boats to train and race against each other during practices helps a team to create a competitive environment and simulate race conditions, and there is nothing like a bit of competition during practice to bring a team up to a higher level.

"Whenever I hear teams out practicing," Vincent Lo now says as he carefully positions a red vinyl maple leaf onto the side of the dragon boat he is finishing, "I always stop to watch." Applying the maple leaf is a special occasion for Lo because it signifies the completion of another boat.

At the moment his attention has been drawn to nearby False Creek where two of his boats are engaged in a race. They are in the middle of what local teams call "bridges," or practice races from one bridge to another. Lo smiles, then says, "It's a great feeling to look out there and know that in my own way I've made a contribution to this sport. What can I say? I love to watch a good race!"

The drum is one of the dragon boat's most distinctive features.

Figureheads Past and Present

Throughout history the figurehead has been an intrinsic part of shipbuilding. No other ship ornamentation, with the possible exception of the sternpiece, has as much superstition, religious ceremony, or symbolism encrusting it. Tracing the genesis of the figurehead, however, is a difficult task, for the majority were made of wood and have since rotted away or lie buried on the ocean floor. Instead, we are left with early pottery paintings, petroglyphs, and more recent discoveries to give us some indications of the original nature of these mystical and symbolic end pieces.

Ancient pottery from the predynastic period (before 3100 BC) in southern Egypt and northern Sudan proves that primitive seacraft were decorated with the skulls of dead animals or human beings. Based on such evidence, it is believed that Neolithic people may have stalked their prey by camouflaging boats with heads and skins of animals.

Humans have been killed for similar reasons, but with a bloody twist. Primitive tribes in various parts of the world have been known to decapitate young female virgins and mount their heads on sticks at the front of their boats. This, they believed, would appease the male god of the sea and ensure a bountiful catch. Blood from the victim, in some cases, would be splashed on the bow, an act anthropologists surmise could be an antecedent to breaking a bottle of champagne on a ship's bow at modern launchings.

Primitive dugout canoes were often identified as personal property by some form of individual carving or painting. Such markings may have led to more detailed engravings on canoes, and later, to decorative figureheads and sternpieces. It is hard to say when the first authentic figureheads originated, but they began appearing on Egyptian vessels as early as 2000 BC. Scandinavian petroglyphs from the Bronze Age (circa 1500 BC) depict ships with elaborate, heavily rockered bows and sterns, which could have been forerunners to later dragon and horse figureheads and sternpieces that terrified the Vikings' victims in the Dark Ages.

One of the earliest known forms of bow ornamentation was the *oculus* or magical eye. The symbol dates back to antiquity and is likely of predynastic Egyptian origin. The *oculus* represented the god Horus and was used to decorate items that accompanied the dead in their burial tombs. Egypt passed the *oculus* on to Phoenicia and the Minoan civilization of Crete which, like the Egyptians, painted *oculi* on the bows of their galleys. From Crete the symbol was probably disseminated throughout the Mediterranean, eventually turning up in Mycenae on the ancient Greek mainland, the later Greek city-states and, of course, Rome itself.

In fact, even today the magical eye surfaces in Mediterranean culture where it can be found on Venetian and Portuguese fishing boats. Once upon a time such a symbol was probably thought necessary to give a boat "eyes" in order to see in the water and thus guarantee good fishing and trading, or a favorable outcome in war. However, contemporary fishermen see it as merely a good-luck charm, possibly to ward off the "evil eye."

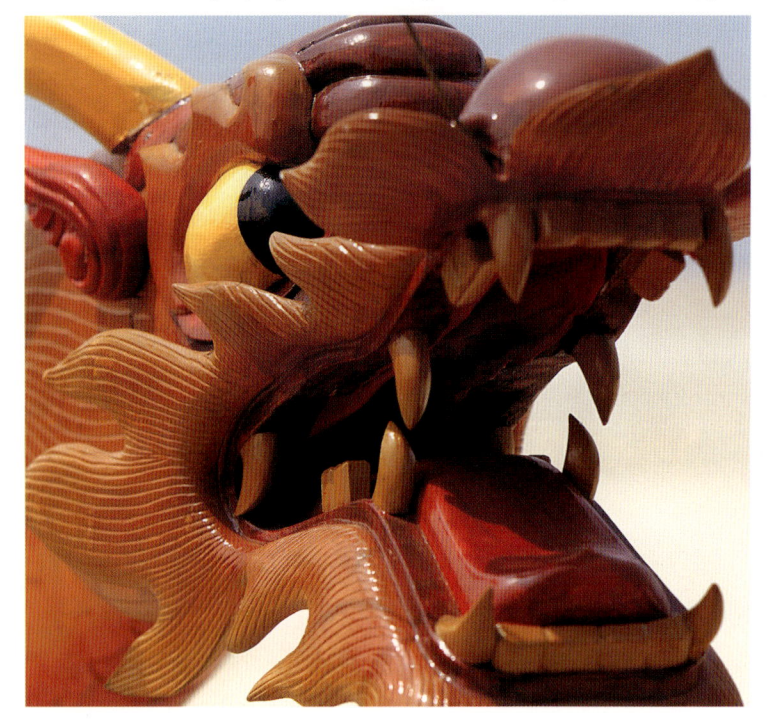

Down through the ages all kinds of devices and symbols have been used to decorate the bows of ships and boats. Ancient seafarers considered the ocean a deity whose temperament ranged from fury to benevolence. Sacrifices to the gods of the oceans were customary throughout much of the ancient world, and the bow of a ship was the best location to make such offerings.

In southwest New Guinea islanders carved likenesses of dead relatives into *bisj* poles at the bows of their boats. It is believed these dead ancestors traveled to the "land of the souls" by means of the pole and the canoe. People from East Borneo carved stem posts for their dugouts into striking representations of snakes similar to the Indian *naga,* while in North Borneo the head of a crocodile, the "demon who eats the unborn child," was used as a figurehead.

The most popular figureheads of an animal, mythical or real, to have graced the prows and sterns of Chinese boats are the dragon and phoenix. Women were forbidden to race in dragon boats in the Hong Kong festival until only recently. The dragon was considered to be characteristically male or yang, so women were made to race in the predominately yin, or female, phoenix boat, which is the same size as a dragon boat.

Figureheads and sternpieces on Maori war canoes are among the most intricately and beautifully carved in all the world. The sternpieces on some of their boats extend 14 or more feet into the air and often take months, sometimes years, to complete. The figurehead is often a highly ornate, birdlike creature with exaggerated eyes, gaping mouth, protruding tongue, and arms extended backward. Known as the god of man and war, this being is positioned at the front of the canoe, warning the god of the ocean of man's presence. Bird feathers arranged on two rods are tied to either side of the figurehead, and feathers also trail in the water from the stern.

Similar to the dragon boat of China, snake boats in India are slender and designed specifically for racing. The boats are heavily gilded with complex carvings usually featuring the *naga,* a creature that appears in Indian epics as a spiritual being that can assume the form of man or snake. As in the Chinese concept of yin and yang, the snake boat represents the two halves of the cosmos: the masculine side as found in the mythical dragon and very real snake and crocodile, and the feminine side as reflected in depictions of heavenly mountains and trees.

In Europe, during the Middle Ages and early Renaissance, depictions of Christian saints became quite popular as figureheads when bows were turned into religious altars. However, as the Reformation swept through England and northern Europe in the 16th and early 17th centuries, such representations of "idols" were banned.

At around the same time, though, shipbuilding and carving entered a golden period as Europe's maritime nations sought to dazzle one another with impressive figureheads on both ships of war and commerce. Leading artists graced bows with fierce lions and dragons or mythological heroes such as Hercules. In the 18th century figurehead carving reached its peak, and an amazing menagerie of creatures – everything from mermaids to minotaurs – sprouted from ships big and small.

Many superstitions were and are associated with seafaring, whether in the extreme as with the custom in ancient Europe of throwing young boys overboard when passing by important headlands, or the great deal less brutal taboos surrounding the act of naming a vessel. Once named, though, a ship could never adopt another sobriquet without inviting certain disaster. The changing of a figurehead, it was believed, could also result in the gravest repercussions. Even mere damage to the ship's proud prow signified future calamity.

By tradition women were thought to bring bad luck to ships, even though seafarers have always invested their vessels with a feminine identity. Female figureheads, on the other hand, were prized as good-luck charms, and bare-breasted examples were considered particularly lucky since they supposedly had the ability to calm the seas, a power no doubt treasured among mariners.

Even before the Industrial Age transformed ships of wood and wind into craft of steel and steam, the figurehead was being supplanted by a rounded bow decorated with scrolls and shields. Today ships and boats of all sizes are still given names, but the sumptuously painted and carved figurehead has gone the route of outlandish hood ornaments so popular on 1950s automobiles. Many contemporary yacht owners have revived the art of figureheads in their own small way, but perhaps it is only in modern dragon boating that one can still glimpse a glorious remnant of what was once a proud and magnificent tradition.

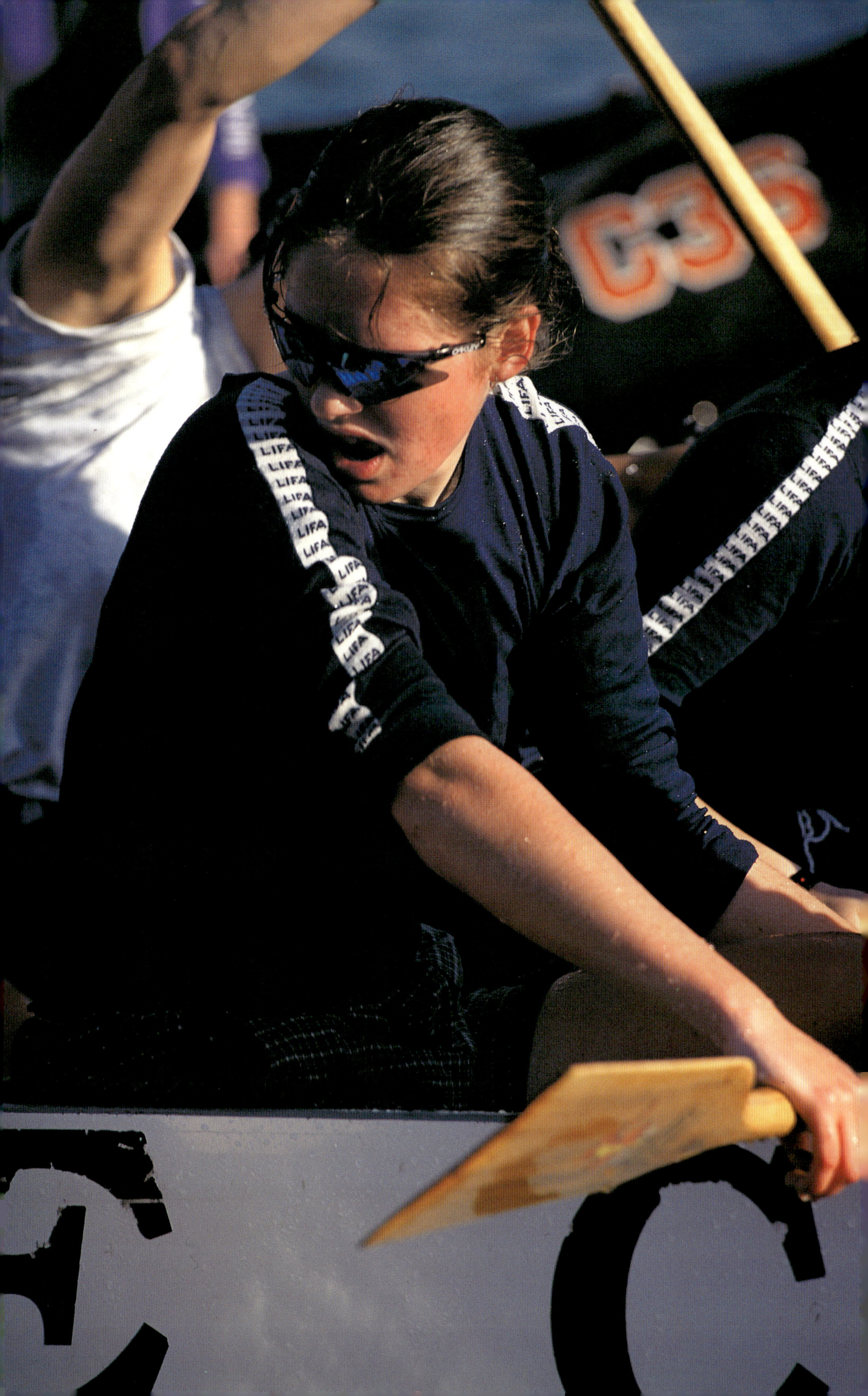
LIFA

3 Paddles Up!

Races and Racers

Paddles poised above the water, 20 men and women wait for what seems like an eternity. Then, finally, the starter roars, "Ready? Go!" and, as if a single mighty being with 40 arms, the dragon boat team responds with a solid first stroke in the water followed by five fully buried strokes that leave their marks in the craft's churning wake. Frantically the drummer shouts, "Up, up, up!" and the racers obey in a furious blur of motion and color. Together, bent in resolute determination, the paddlers glide across the water, not one paddle too fast, nor one too slow. And then, seemingly in a blink of an eye, the practice race is over and the drummer cries out, "Paddles up!" Instantly the team members react in military fashion, raising their paddles in perfect unison, anticipating yet another start in what has already been a long day of training.

Knowing others is wisdom;
Knowing the self is enlightenment.
Mastering others requires force;
Mastering the self needs strength.

The Club

Hugh Fisher was a medical student at the University of British Columbia the year Rene Roddick asked him about paddling clubs. Roddick, a marathon canoeist from Vancouver, had been making trips out to Burnaby Lake to paddle and admits to being awed by Fisher during that first encounter. "I remember meeting this guy who had won gold and bronze medals in kayaking at the 1984 Los Angeles Olympics. I thought that was pretty exciting. We were introduced and we just started talking about paddling."

Being great, it flows.
It flows far away.
Having gone far, it returns.

Fisher caught Roddick's enthusiasm and suggested that if he and his friends were really interested in paddling, they should start up their own club. Roddick acted on Fisher's suggestion and, in a quest for a suitable location for the club, organized a meeting with the False

Amy Whiffin, one of the members of Vancouver's False Creek Women's Dragon Boat Team, pauses to rest during an interval session.

As seen from Vancouver's Cambie Street Bridge, a dragon boat team slices through the waters of False Creek during a training session.

Creek Community Centre's board of directors.

Fortunately for the group of paddlers, Carol Sogawa, the coordinator of the community center, recognized the project as a worthwhile venture and helped make the dream come true. The group managed to find an unused storage shed in front of the community center, and Roddick told Fisher the good news. Fisher then contacted some of his friends in the paddling community, and the False Creek Racing Canoe Club (FCRCC) was born.

"To start with," Fisher now recalls, "we needed a piece of water, a building, boats, and people. False Creek had the water and the space, and we had the people, but it wasn't all hooked together. I knew that if I wanted to paddle in a club I'd have to put one together."

Fisher is pragmatic about his reasons for helping to set up the FCRCC. "As a group, we recognized that there were lots of different ways of paddling a boat forward. By providing a facility to train out of, we could expose a number of people to all the other paddling sports. Fortuitously Expo 86 provided a way for all of these paddlers to paddle together in the same boat."

Hong Kong had presented six teak dragon boats to Vancouver as part of the 1986 world's fair's transportation-and-communication theme. "We had," says Fisher, "a number of people from various canoeing backgrounds coming together to train for one common goal – winning a trip to Hong Kong. However, at that point, we knew nothing about dragon boating."

Fisher says that the sport of dragon boating achieved instant popularity because athletes were successful at it right away. He jokingly describes it as "the lowest form of canoeing known to man." But this, he adds, is the reason it has become so popular: "Anyone can do it. It's fun to do and it has all the social aspects of what's fun in sport. Technically it's very simple."

The champion kayaker feels that dragon boating is an excellent entry-level activity for canoeing. "It's the place to start, especially with school kids. You learn the absolute basics of the canoe stroke in dragon boating. Hopefully it opens kids' eyes to other canoe sports."

The False Creek Racing Canoe Club became instantly successful as a result of a few people, mostly volunteers, who happened to share the same vision. There were only 20 people in the club in those first few months; today 67 dragon boat teams and 36 outrigger crews train and race there.

The Team

One of the most attractive features of dragon boating is that it can be enjoyed purely as a recreational pastime while still satisfying even the most dedicated athlete interested in world-caliber competition. Peter Liljedahl, who coaches a group of high school paddlers in Vancouver, puts it best: "Dragon boating can take a person who perhaps has never really excelled at anything and make him or her part of a really good team."

Liljedahl, who comes from an elite paddling background, has been involved with dragon boating in Vancouver since 1986 and has coached at the junior level for the past three years. He is a firm believer in downplaying results while emphasizing process. "This is not to say," he adds, "that I tell the juniors they can't win a race. Instead I tell them, 'Winning is in your grasp, but you'll have to have the best race of your lives to do it.' These kids don't need motivation. They're keyed up already. Rarely do I have to motivate them. It's getting them to focus on the race plan that is the most challenging thing."

That which shrinks
Must first expand.
That which fails
Must first be strong.

Vancouver also boasts one of the most successful dragon boat teams in the world. Over the past seven years the False Creek Women's Dragon Boat Team has picked up medals, including five golds, at every Hong Kong international competition it has attended. At the 1995 Hong Kong Dragon Boat Festival the team struck gold, while in Yueyang, China, the same year, it brought home three silver medals.

What is the secret to this kind of success? No doubt most coaches would say training, training, and more training, as well as the constant honing of technique, consummate teamwork, and the ability to focus both body and soul on propelling the boat forward to the finish line.

Heather Taylor, a champion marathon paddler, was one of the founding members of the False Creek Racing Canoe Club. She first started dragon boat training with the False Creek men's team, which was originally a mixed crew. However, when the men discovered that free air trips to Hong Kong were being awarded to the top men's team, Taylor and a few other women soon found themselves onshore without a crew.

"In retrospect," recalls Taylor, "although I was disappointed at the time, it was better for us in the long run." Without wasting much time Taylor began enlisting paddlers by putting up notices at swimming pools and fitness clubs.

"In March 1986 I got a call from Heather," says Alison Hart, a 10-year veteran with the False Creek women's team. "She was phoning every woman she knew who had a paddling history. The ripple effect brought in even more people, and within a couple of weeks we were on the water three times a week. And just like that a team was born!"

Mary Anne Purdy, who has worn two hats over the past two decades as both paddler and coach, recalls that "We started out with bent-shaft paddles [used in marathon canoeing] and we tried to adapt the marathon canoe stroke to the voyageur canoes we were training in. I'd never been in a canoe so big, and I can remember being out on the water and thinking how awkward these boats were to paddle and steer."

In those early years of training, the members of the False Creek women's team suffered bruised and bloodied hips from bracing against the sides of the voyageur canoes. "The boats were difficult to get the balance right in," says Purdy. "But all of this was more a learning process for us rather than the fault of the boats. We were using them for something they weren't really designed for."

The women of False Creek have come a long way since those formative years, but dragon boating is not just about winning medals. Don Irvine, co-owner of Six-Sixteen Dragon Boats and the coach of the False Creek women's team from 1987 to 1993, echoes Hugh Fisher's sentiments about the accessibility of the sport: "The most important lesson I ever learned coaching dragon boaters was not to write someone off early. I thought one paddler I coached would never make

The False Creek women's team training at the First World Championships in Yueyang in 1995.

the team. After two years of perseverance, though, she not only made the team, but was up there in the top five or six paddlers. If given a chance, it's amazing what people can do in this sport."

A dragon boat team consists of a steersperson, a drummer, and 20 individual paddling units. The steersperson finds the straightest course possible, while the drummer provides a crew's timing and motivation. The paddlers, naturally, are the boat's engine.

Every seat in the dragon boat is as important as the next to propel the vessel quickly across a racecourse, but probably no one has quite the responsibility that the steersperson has. The pressure of keeping the boat on course during the race can be an intimidating force when experienced for the first time.

Some steerspeople prefer to stand in the boat so that they can use their bodies as braces against the 20-foot steering oar and project their voices more easily down the boat. While these people favor a higher vantage point, others find more comfort and control sitting down. "Steering is a real 'feeling,'" says Anne-Marie Nehring, veteran steersperson for the False Creek women's team. "The most important thing," she adds, "is to keep looking ahead and focus on an object down the course. You have to make sure that the nose of the boat stays on that object, and you must never look back to steer."

Nehring says that when she's steering she keeps the blade of the

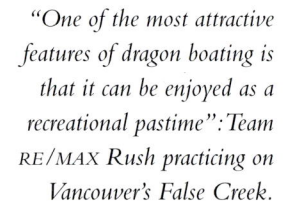

"One of the most attractive features of dragon boating is that it can be enjoyed as a recreational pastime": Team RE/MAX Rush practicing on Vancouver's False Creek.

oar out of the water as much as possible. This method results in the least amount of resistance as the boat glides along the water. She does, however, keep the oar hovering, ready to plunge it back in instantly if the boat begins to veer off course.

The strategy employed by the steersperson depends entirely on the dynamics of the water. In Hong Kong, for instance, the racecourse is turbulent and often unpredictable, which requires the steersperson to maintain constant contact with the water. In Vancouver's False Creek, where the water is much flatter and therefore more predictable, steering is not quite as difficult. On the other hand, a course such as the one in Yueyang, China, is generally even flatter and calmer, which means the steersperson can keep the oar out of the water during most of the race.

During a race, the drummer and steersperson have command of the boat from the moment the team pushes away from the dock, but for some paddlers it is the drummer who becomes the entire focus of their race. In moments of fatigue or faltering confidence, the drummer can become a profound source of inspiration.

From the shore it would appear that it is the drummer who sets a dragon boat's pace. That job, though, belongs to the strokes, the two paddlers at the front of the boat. The drummer, in effect, bangs the drum at the same time, or just slightly ahead, of the strokes' paddles hitting the water. It is the front-seat paddlers whom the drummer will key on for the duration of the race, all the while keeping an eye on the rest of the paddlers in the boat.

When the stroke paddlers' top hands are raised high, the drummer's hands mirror them; when their arms come down, the drummer's arms also descend. Many drummers find this technique to be an effective way of maintaining the timing and focus of the team. In a sense, the drummer becomes the heartbeat of the dragon boat.

Another aspect of dragon boating that makes it particularly attractive for the neophyte and experienced competitor alike is the relative lack of equipment necessary to participate. Festivals, of course, provide the boats, paddles, drums, and steering oars for races, while clubs may or may not supply all these things for practices, but there are a few things a prospective dragon boater will definitely need to acquire on his or her own.

Although it is difficult to get really *comfortable* in a dragon boat, there are a few purchases a paddler can make to ease the pain. First and foremost is a bum pad, which can be custom-made out of foam or Thinsulate from a camping store. Clothing is an area of great concern, especially for paddlers who practice year-round. Even in Vancouver's

DRAGON BOATS: A CELEBRATION

A steersperson perched high on a traditional long dragon boat in Yueyang, China.

moderate climate the more serious teams can expect ice at least a few weeks out of every year. Cold-weather paddling practically demands layered clothing, which is a proven insulator against the cold.

Polypropylene or silk underwear is ideal as a first layer; such materials have remarkable abilities to wick perspiration away from the body. Cotton T-shirts are not recommended as first layers, since cotton next to the skin actually robs the body of heat and remains cold when wet. The middle layer serves as an insulator, therefore, the colder it is outside, the more layers required. Keep in mind that you can always strip down if too hot. As for the outer layer, polypropylene turtlenecks and fleece jackets are popular for really cold days, while fleece pants act as an insulator between the dragon boat seat and the paddler's bottom.

Another item worth investing in is a rain suit. Breathable fabric is

46

An Australian drummer waves her country's flag during the closing ceremonies at the First World Championships in Yueyang.

preferred, but inexpensive nylon will do the trick. Even on the clearest of days it is worth taking a jacket into the boat. Inevitably each paddler will be splashed repeatedly by someone else's paddle. Besides, the weather can easily change in a two-hour practice, or you might find yourself sitting still during periods of instruction.

In the early years of dragon boating in Vancouver inventive gear was often employed by various paddlers to withstand cold-weather practices. The more memorable solutions for surviving frigid temperatures and the resulting effect on the extremities included paddling with dishwashing gloves, placing plastic bags over hiking boots, and, on one memorable occasion, sporting a fluorescent-orange bathing cap.

Today "poggies" are a must. Available in neoprene or lightweight nylon, poggies resemble a mitten that opens at the fingertips, encircles the paddle shaft, and attaches with Velcro. The advantage of poggies over other kinds of gloves is that the hands stay in constant contact with the paddle and are protected from the rain, wind, and spray from other teammates' paddles. However, neoprene poggies tend to get hotter and sweatier than nylon ones, resulting in blisters.

Neoprene wet suits, especially leggings, are great for cold-weather paddling. Neoprene has the ability to trap a thin layer of water between its skintight fabric and a paddler's skin. The neoprene is then warmed by the body which, in the end, is insulated from the cold. Paddling jackets are ideal in that they use cuff and neck seals to guard against the chilling effects of water and spray. And if your coach doesn't

The False Creek men's team regroups after the men's final in Hong Kong.

Looking for the ultimate "trader" at Vancouver's dragon boat festival.

keep you sitting around for long periods of time, windproof nylon shells also work just fine. Finally, since 85 percent of heat is lost through the head, it is advisable in cold weather to keep that part of the body covered, something cross-country ski toques or baseball caps do reasonably well.

Warm-weather paddling requires less gear, but adequate protection should still be taken against the sun. Footwear can include anything from river sandals and running shoes to aqua socks and bare feet, but make certain you rinse salt water from your gear, especially running shoes, which can smell pretty bad after a few practices. On those hot days of summer, spandex cycling shorts are great, especially the ones with neoprene bottoms sewn into them. Tank tops are fine for the top, but it never hurts to bring along an extra long-sleeved top, not to mention plenty of sunscreen.

Swapping or trading uniforms has become an official "unscheduled" event of every dragon boat race. Athletes can be seen stripping down right after the finals to get their favorite "traders," as they are often called. During the races, teams are, of course, identified by their individual uniforms, but by the end of a festival the members of each team are usually a rainbow of multinational colors from opposing clubs, sporting shorts, hats, shirts, jackets, and pants acquired from fellow competitors.

The Technique

Finding the exact combination of timing, power, and stamina required to make a dragon boat fly across the water takes perseverance and practice. Solid teamwork is of utmost importance in achieving such success, but the ability to master all the components of the dragon boat stroke is paramount. The three goals of good technique are coordination of the timing of all 20 paddling units, thus maximizing the speed of the boat; maximization in a forward direction of the force generated by each paddling unit; and minimization of all forces generated by each paddling unit in any other direction.

To accomplish these goals, good technique works on three principles: timing, power, and efficiency. However, of all the components in dragon boat racing, timing is the most important. At the world championship level there are crews comprised of different shapes, sizes, and techniques, but what characterizes all the winners is perfect timing, something that is only achieved after long hours of training together on the water, plenty of timing drills, and learning to feel the surge and glide of the boat and tap into its innate rhythm.

Seeing the small is insight;
Yielding to force is strength.
Using the outer light, return to insight,
And in this way be saved from harm.

Stroke length, stroke rate, and stroke intensity are three important technique variables. Every paddler has his or her own optimum stroke rate, length, and intensity. However, with 20 paddlers in a dragon boat, not everyone's technique will be one that the entire team can emulate. It is the essence of dragon boating that individual efforts contribute to the boat's performance. Therefore, overreaching, pulling too hard or recovering too quickly (better known as "doing your own thing"), will result in timing errors and affect the group's performance. Mastering timing and the basics of stroke mechanics are crucial to achieving maximum boat speed.

There are six key parts to the dragon boat stroke. When done properly, a boat flies; when executed improperly, the boat will feel sluggish and heavy. The first three components set up the stroke, while the last three are considered to be the work-phase part of the stroke. The six components are called: rotation, reach/extension, catch, pull, exit, and recovery.

An image used by some coaches to help paddlers picture rotation is to imagine that a pole is inserted through the head, along the spine, and then anchored to the dragon boat seat. A paddler's head, shoulders, and torso should feel as if they are rotated around this pole until the upper body is fully extended. Another way to think of achieving

The False Creek women's team "recovering" together during a practice session.

DRAGON BOATS: A CELEBRATION

full rotation is to present your back to the shore, or have your chest facing your partner. The goal is to attain sufficient torso rotation so that reach/extension can be maximized, which allows for the recruitment of most of the muscles in the back and hip region. However, the paddler's body should be relaxed while rotating, a difficult thing to achieve with such an awkward position.

Reach/extension is crucial in maximizing the length of the stroke. Ideally the reach of each paddler should be consistent throughout the boat. Besides timing, reach is the first thing that suffers when the stroke rate gets too high, or the fitness of the paddlers is too low. There has to be an extension of the outside shoulder, which begins during the rotation phase. Imagine a rubber band stretching and you will have an idea of what should happen to the shoulder as it brings the paddle through, relaxed and ready for the work load. The outside shoulder is then "dropped," which means that once the paddle is fully extended it reaches out a few extra inches by both extending and lowering the shoulder.

A blur of color and speed characterize dragon boating at its most exciting.

Although all the components of the dragon boat stroke are important, catch, the moment when the blade first bites into the water, is critical to the speed of the craft. The top arm is held out over the water while the top hand is approximately six inches away from the forehead or face. This achieves two things: it sets up the blade in the correct position to load it up with water, and, by keeping the top hand fairly close to the forehead, it allows the paddler to avoid "lifting" (the displacement of water upward instead of backward). The top hand then drives down on the paddle, while the bottom arm relaxes at the shoulder and allows the top arm to drive the paddle downward. The hand should maintain its position in front of the forehead through the pull and exit phase.

Once all 20 paddles are submerged and outside arms are fully extended, the next component of the stroke, pull, occurs. Paddles are pulled back directly parallel with the boat so that the blade of the paddle is perfectly square for maximum resistance. The top arm drive stabilizes the paddle as the bottom arm and back muscles pull the paddle back. In executing pull it is important to remember that at this point the stroke is dominated by trunk rotation. Maximum power and endurance will come from using the larger muscles of the back, shoulders, and trunk rather than relying on the smaller arm muscles. The arms simply transfer this power to the paddle. Only when the blade is anchored (i.e., when catch has been initiated and the blade of the paddle has been loaded up with water) can the paddler move into pull. Remember, when initiating pull, that the blade must be fully buried and stay directly perpendicular to the boat. It is the water out in front that must be moved.

The most effective stroke is achieved by de-rotating the torso while pulling back. If the arm is bent while pulling backward, it is likely that the wrong muscles are being used and full efficiency will not be realized. Everything that is done in the stroke should be conducive to propelling the boat forward. Any energy moving out to the side or up and down is basically wasted energy and will not assist in maximizing boat speed. This includes unnecessary "bobbing," which occurs when a paddler incorrectly achieves reach or rotation due to bending at the waist.

At the end of the stroke the paddle should exit the water midway between the knee and hip cleanly and quickly. When the blade exits the water at about mid-thigh, the arm bends slightly to allow the paddle to clear the water and then is pushed or snapped forward.

Finally recovery describes what happens to the paddle once it has gone through the work phase and is preparing for another stroke. But

The dragon boat stroke:
A. *reach/extension;* B. *catch;*
C. *and* D. *pull;* E. *exit.*

A.

B.

C.

D.

E.

don't let the term be misleading, for although the paddler enters a rest phase when muscles aren't working as hard, recovery speed plays a large role in determining stroke rate. With an average rate of 84 strokes per minute during a race, or the even more blistering 120 of Chinese and Indonesian teams during a race finish, such a pace would be impossible without a speedy recovery.

Recovery occurs quickly, but it is still important to keep the body position relaxed, even momentarily. During recovery, the strong rotation muscles of the back are stretched forward, thus "winding up the spring" for catch and pull. It is especially important to have a relaxed grip on the paddle during recovery to avoid muscle cramping. Of course, staying relaxed is probably the most difficult part of the stroke. It is hard not to feel like a sardine when you are wedged into a dragon boat with 21 other people. As Olympian Hugh Fisher says, "Just do this 100,000 times and you'll start to get it right!"

There are three additional dragon boat strokes that are used to maneuver the craft. These strokes are known as back paddling, the draw stroke, and the pry stroke.

Back paddling is used most often when bringing the boat into or away from the loading dock. It is also an important stroke for holding the boat steady at the start of a race, or for maneuvering the boat backward at the start line. Back paddling is done by holding the paddle at an angle behind you and pulling the water there toward the front of the boat.

The draw stroke is used by the paddlers in the front or back to line up the boat straight at the start of a race and to turn the boat around. Sometimes it is used by one whole side of the boat at once, for example, when docking the boat. The draw stroke is achieved by reaching out perpendicular to the side of the boat and pulling the water toward you, which in turn will move the craft in the direction of the paddle. Make sure that the flat part of the paddle is facing you.

The pry, or pushaway, stroke can be combined with the draw for faster maneuvering when lining up the boat or drawing the boat over to one side. It is usually done opposite the person who is drawing the boat. The technique involves sticking the paddle straight up and down against the boat's side, with the blade flat against the hull. The top hand then pulls the top of the paddle down toward the inside of the boat while the heel of the bottom hand acts as a buffer against the boat's side. The pry stroke disperses water up and out to the side, moving the vessel away from the paddle. It is possible to use the side of the boat as a fulcrum and the paddle as a lever. However, this practice can cause damage to the boat's side as well as to the paddle.

Overhead view of paddlers during the pull phase of the dragon boat stroke.

Stroke rate describes the frequency or number of strokes per minute. Rates are monitored during both training and racing, and every crew has its own magic number. In the early years of international competitions in Hong Kong, stroke rates varied from the low sixties to more than 120 strokes per minute. The standard paddle length for dragon boating is relatively short, so higher stroke rates than those usually found in outrigger canoeing can be maintained. On average, competitive dragon boat teams paddle at a rate of about 82 strokes per minute. Different body types can influence the rate: the smaller, slightly built team may opt for a faster rate, while the taller, bigger teams may find a longer, powerful stroke more effective.

Some teams vary their stroke rate during the race, beginning with a faster rate to bring the boat out of a dead start. Once the boat is up to race speed the team will reach out and often keep the rate at a solid 82 strokes per minute until the drummer calls a finish. The drummer usually calls the finish somewhere near the end of the racecourse (approximately 100 meters) to let the team know it has only a short distance left to go, or when the race is particularly close between boats and it is necessary to put on one last surge.

Stroke rates are worth experimenting with, since every team is made up of paddlers with different fitness levels and abilities. By experimenting with the stroke rate during training and racing, a team will eventually find a rate that suits its level.

The Training

Training for Vancouver's False Creek women's and men's teams usually begins in November and lasts until the international competitions in Hong Kong and China, which are usually held sometime in June, depending on the Chinese calendar. The weather on Canada's West Coast allows athletes the luxury of year-round training, although for a short time in winter teams may still have to endure icy conditions.

Teams such as Vancouver's RE/MAX Rush, which races in the recreational division, begin training in January with three or four practices a week. Although RE/MAX Rush doesn't train at the level of the False Creek women's team, it still takes its training and racing seriously. "We wouldn't be out there at 6:00 a.m. if we *weren't* serious," claims realtor and captain Sarina McKenzie.

In the early months of training, crews such as the False Creek women's team are on the water two or three times per week, with an additional workout added in January. Weight training begins in October, usually after the last outrigger race of the season. Many of the teams in Vancouver paddle dragon boats in the winter and spring, then move to outriggers in the summer.

Weights and paddling are supplemented by additional aerobic workouts such as running, cycling, or cross-country skiing. Added to these activities are rigorous fitness tests and time trials that are held monthly. All in all, dragon boaters spend a lot of time training.

A fitness test involves a timed run that varies from a distance of approximately 3,000 meters in the early months to 800 meters later in the season. The 800-meter run, in particular, approximates the time of an actual dragon boat race. Such distances help to ascertain the aerobic capacity and general cardiovascular fitness of a team. The other component of the fitness test, performed in a local fitness club, assesses an individual's strength and endurance. Here the team is tested with a number of exercises, including bench press, bench pulls, chin-ups, dips, and sit-ups.

In addition to resistance training in the weight room, which develops general strength, power, and endurance, there are specific drills that can be done in the dragon boat itself. This is achieved by having part of the team paddle while the remainder rests. Resistance training in the dragon boat is an excellent way of overloading the muscles specifically used in paddling.

Yield and overcome;
Bend and be straight;
Empty and be full;
Wear out and be new.

Another method of applying resistance is to drag an old tire behind the boat. This procedure is considered "heavy" resistance, especially when training with a smaller number of paddlers than the usual 20. Needless to say, it should be used sparingly. Another, "lighter" way of applying resistance is to tie a boat buoy or bumper under the vessel. The buoy provides enough resistance to hinder the boat's glide without putting undue strain on the athletes' joints and muscles.

In emphasizing the resistance on the paddle stroke, such exercises reinforce the catch and pull phases and provide instant feedback to the team. Light resistance training forces the stroke rate to be lowered, helping athletes to focus on timing and technique. The general rule is that if a crew member can't paddle well slowly, he or she can't paddle well fast. In other words, mistakes made at a slow rate are only magnified when paddling at a faster rate.

Seat pulls are another form of resistance training in which two or more team members pull the weight of the dragon boat by paddling the entire craft by themselves. This type of training is also a good way to add variety to a practice, since the coach can choose a number of seat combinations, interval times, and effort – front half, back half, single seats only, alternating seats, et cetera.

By overloading his or her muscles, a paddler can achieve a greater training effect and ultimately make the boat move faster. Along with challenging one's self physically, it is critical to develop the neuro-muscular system (or "feel") so that the application of force can be maximized. As each individual gets a better "feel," so does the whole crew through the catch phase of the stroke, which makes the boat go fast, and the pull phase, which maintains the craft's speed.

Interval training is the foundation for all dragon boat practices. This kind of training builds speed endurance and anaerobic fitness by alternating predetermined periods of hard paddling with intervals of rest or easy paddling. Often interval training involves taking a portion of the distance being trained for, say, a three-minute racecourse, and dividing that time into shorter periods. These segments of hard work, combined with short rest periods, challenge the endurance system while developing speed and power. An example of speed-endurance intervals would be one minute of hard paddling followed by one minute of easy paddling.

The rewards of physical training can be reflected in the enhanced athletic prowess and technical proficiency of a team. What is often overlooked, however, is the importance of preparing a team psychologically

Chris Grunow of the False Creek Men's Dragon Boat Team warms up before a race in Hong Kong.

One last stretch for Lori Stewart, a member of the False Creek women's team, prior to a race in Yueyang.

for racing. As Canadian sport psychologist Terry Orlick has written, "In sport, mental imagery is used primarily to help you get the best out of yourself in training and competition. The developing athletes who make the fastest progress and those who ultimately perform at their best make extensive use of mental imagery. They use it daily as a means of directing what will happen in training and as a way of pre-experiencing their best competition performances."

A team's ability to focus on the task at hand is extremely important. "Commitment and self-control," Orlick writes, "are thought to be the keys to excellence. In order to excel in any field you must be committed, but you also need enough self-control to perform well under a variety of circumstances." Perhaps former basketball player Kareem Abdul Jabbar summed it up best when he said, "You have to be able to center yourself, to let all of your emotions go. Don't ever forget that you play with your soul as well as your body."

Every group of people has its own goal when forming a dragon boat team. Some enjoy the routine and fitness opportunities that paddling offers, while others prize the social camaraderie involved with a group. And then there are those who take pleasure in the exhilaration of training and the challenge of competitive racing.

The Race

For some paddlers, racing becomes the reward for all the long hours put into training. In the early days many Vancouver dragon boat teams trained six or seven months to compete in just two races, or approximately six minutes of racing in the entire year! With the increasing worldwide popularity of the sport, however, a truly serious competitive dragon boat team can now look forward to festivals and races on four continents year-round.

Race starts vary from one festival to the next. In Hong Kong's Victoria Harbour teams back up their boats close to Chinese junks that are assigned to each lane. Then the steersperson is handed a long tethered rope attached to a junk. This rope must be held until the horn is sounded at the start of the race. In Yueyang, China, on the other hand, dragon boaters back-paddle into a starting barrack with a mechanized steel vise that holds the boat until the start of the race. Unlike most dragon boat competitions in other countries, the races in Yueyang

Visualization exercises are an important component of dragon boat training. Here the False Creek women's team simulates a race before the actual event in Yueyang.

don't allow paddles to touch the water until the start gun is fired.

The races in Vancouver's Canadian International Dragon Boat Festival use buoys to separate eight race lanes. Two ropes are employed at the start line — one across the front of the boats and one behind them. In a sense, the boats are "roped in" at the start. Each team is allowed one false start; however, a second false start by the same boat results in immediate disqualification.

A referee is responsible for the preliminary aligning of the boats and then passes control of the race to the starter, who instructs crews to move up to the start line and remain there. When the crews are properly lined up, the starter gives the starting command, followed a few seconds later by a loud cannon blast. Some races may replace the cannon blast with the honk of a starter's horn, a gunshot, or some other distinct sound.

Once the steersperson has let go of the rope each team is left to its own devices to get down the racecourse as quickly as possible. Over the years many teams have experimented with their starts. Some teams employ a start known as "6-16," which was coined and developed by Don Irvine and Drew Mitchell.

The basic idea of the start is to get the boat up and moving to race speed as quickly as humanly possible. Obviously the boat that achieves the fastest start will have an immediate psychological advantage. The "six" of the phrase "6-16" refers to six hard, powerful strokes that propel the deadweight of the dragon boat forward. Paddles are extended but not locked straight out. In effect, three-quarters of the paddle blade is buried in the water on the first stroke. Through the next five strokes the paddle is buried deeper so that by the sixth the boat should be moving quite quickly. The stroke rate is then significantly increased for 16 accelerated strokes with the goal of reaching top speed at the 16th and settling into the racing stroke rate.

. . . the sage is sharp but not cutting,
Pointed but not piercing,
Straightforward but not unrestrained,
Brilliant but not blinding.

The finish is usually called by the drummer and consists of a final effort during the last 40 to 60 strokes of a race. The drummer may command the finish earlier if a race is particularly tight, but the chief idea of his or her call is to channel every reserve a team may possibly have into the final strokes. After more than two minutes of all-out paddling, the drummer's shout for the finish may well be music to aching arms.

After the race is over, crew members thrust their paddles into the air to signal completion. For one team completion means victory, but every team shares the personal goal of throwing body and soul into an athletic endeavor, something that can be seen in the faces of all dragon boaters as they embrace and congratulate their fellow paddlers.

A race start at the Hong Kong Dragon Boat Festival in 1995.

*The moment of truth after a close race. The False Creek women's team
discovers it has indeed won gold in Hong Kong in 1995.*

White Light, Power Animals, and *Wu*

Curiously, even today, many Chinese believe that the dragon boat festival falls on one of the unluckiest days of the year, a time when yin and yang are in conflict, evil is on the loose, and demons are to be found everywhere. It is not surprising then that numerous superstitions and rituals have come to be associated with the Festival of the Double Fifth. Much of the original fertility aspects of the festival have fallen into disuse, and certainly humans are no longer sacrificed, but over the centuries a whole series of rituals and rites were devised by the Chinese to combat the malignant influences threatening them at such an important time of the year. In effect, high noon in China on the double fifth became the critical moment to protect oneself from any number of reversals of fortune.

Wu, a homonym for the number five, is a recurring element in the rites and rituals connected to the dragon boat festival. According to ancient Chinese beliefs dating back to the Zhou dynasty (1122–256 BC), the universe is driven by two systems: yin and yang, the balancing of the female/negative with the male/positive; and the *wu hing,* or five-agent system, which teaches that everything in the world is influenced by one of five elements – wood, earth, fire, metal, and water. These two systems, it is said, are connected with each other by the agent of the earth, which holds a neutral position. Furthermore, the agents of wood and fire are dominated by yang, while the agents of metal and water are ruled by yin.

"Fiveness" can still be found in many aspects of the dragon boat festival. Clothes are embroidered with the images of the five poisonous animals – snake, centipede, toad, scorpion, lizard – which are thought to ward off negative influences. Five colors – red/fire, blue/wood, yellow/earth, white/metal, and black/water – predominate in the festival. Red, particularly, is found in abundance since *wu* has a close relationship with this color. Five is the male number and red/fire is quintessentially male and extremely useful in combating negative influences.

In fact, there are a whole series of *wu* practices one can employ for protection: tying five different colored strands into the hair of young children; eating Chinese dumplings wrapped with five-colored strands; placing a five-colored paper charm under the bed; and eating soup made from beans of five different colors.

Today, especially in sports, superstitions can still play an important role in the performance of athletes. In dragon boat racing, psyching up 22 people before a race, or rechanneling the fear of competition, has led to the development of some unique rituals and superstitions.

"There's probably nothing scarier than sitting at the start line at a world championship," says Anne-Marie Nehring, steersperson and spiritual leader of the False Creek Women's Dragon Boat Team. Nehring helps the team rechannel its fears and focus on the race plan by practicing "white light" before every race. Crew members huddle in a circle, and Nehring calmly has them imagine that they are in their boat and are surrounded by a protective white light. She tells the team how important it is to eliminate negative thoughts, such as beating the other teams, and urges it to return to a more spiritual realm. "As soon as you move into that unlimited place, everything becomes one," Nehring explains. In order to achieve that place, Nehring has the team's members recite various chants.

In addition to white light, Nehring has also provided each member of the team with a "power animal." Says Nehring: "The power animals give each athlete an identity." She explains that in every competitor it is the inner child that becomes the most scared and vulnerable. "The power animals are comforting," she further notes. "They keep us in touch with the bigger spirit in all of us."

Nehring came across the concept of power animals when she was taking a course on shamanism. Each team member receives her animal through a series of questions, and a small crystal is then used to determine which animal an athlete will get. "Coincidentally," Nehring adds, "most team members are water animals. We have many dolphins, a few seals, killer whales, and a beluga whale. But we also have a hummingbird, a black bear, and an eagle."

Another ritual practiced by many local Vancouver crews involves an active visualization of the entire race. Sitting in race formation on the ground, the drummer sets her watch for the team's estimated race time and calls out commands. Meanwhile the team responds by physically acting out the stroke and the race plan.

Similar to the power animal, but on a more humorous level, are the "power patches" of a team from Vancouver that calls itself the Dragon Ladies. While in China the team's two coaches adapted an old professional hockey tradition of sporting beards when a team makes the National Hockey League playoffs. In lieu of beards, the Dragon Ladies left unshaven patches of hair somewhere on their bodies until after the final race.

The "ritual to the tree" is yet another ceremony the Dragon Ladies perform prior to each race. "When possible," says Coach Paul Dever, "the team surrounds a tree. Otherwise anything made of wood will do." Dever then takes his place in the center of the group and assumes the role of spiritual leader. Circling the tree, he gives a sermon that has something of a religious quality to it. He thanks the tree for the wood used in the team's dragon boat and paddles, then asks the tree to give each crew member strength in the coming race.

When Dever was unable to attend the races in Yueyang, China, in 1995, the Dragon Ladies asked him to shave off his beard and give it to the team. The resulting bag of hair accompanied the team to China, and in Dever's absence the hair was used in the ritual to the tree.

When asked about the rituals and superstitions involved in dragon boat racing, Kathryn Reid of the False Creek mixed team describes a "total bonding thing that happens when you're part of a team. There's also something primitive about the sport."

Just watching one of New Zealand's many dragon boat teams perform a *haka* makes one realize what Reid means. The *haka,* a traditional Maori war dance of ancient times, serves as both a spiritual bonding for the group and as a dance meant to intimidate the enemy. The tradition, which has survived centuries, serves the same purpose today, and observing a New Zealand dragon boat team performing it conjures up images of past Maori warriors with intricate body tattoos, bulging eyes, and extruded tongues. The fierce chanting and violent movements that accompany a *haka* are guaranteed to unnerve the opposition while creating a psychological bond among team members.

Lately tattooing and body painting have become popular with some dragon boaters. "We did it as an act of team bonding," says Lori Stewart, one of nine members of the False Creek women's team who sport tattoos. She explains that three of her teammates made a pact that they would get tattoos if they made the False Creek team. After that, people (including herself) she "never thought would do it" suddenly put permanent symbols on their bodies.

Less-permanent rituals include stick-on tattoos, face painting, and the shaving of national emblems into heads. The latter is more common among men's teams, who style their hair into a bit of national pride. Maps of Australia, the Canadian flag, and abbreviations for countries such as SWE and NZ are common on the crowns of dragon boaters at international festivals. Similar rites and ceremonies were practiced in ancient China by the tribes of the south who worshipped the dragon as their totem. On the Festival of the Double Fifth these people shaved their heads and tattooed the motif of the dragon on their bodies. Such acts, combined with the races themselves, were thought to appease the dragons who brought about life-giving rains.

Today many people indulge in superstitions and customs without really knowing how ancient their roots are. One such common practice is the splashing of water on one another after a dragon boat race. This ritual may well be connected to the Chinese Water Sprinkling Festival, an important celebration of the Dai people of southern China.

According to legend, China was ruled by an evil King of Fire who kept seven beautiful young sisters prisoner. One day the youngest of the seven discovered a method to kill the king, which he mistakenly told her while drunk. In his stupor the king confessed that the only way to eliminate him was to cut off his head with a strand of hair from his scalp. The young woman carried out the deed, but when she tried to dispose of the king's head, every path she crossed caught fire. Soon the entire village was ablaze, and when she tried to return the head, she, too, was set on fire. However, her sisters rushed to her aid and eventually put out the fire. From then on the Dai lived in peace and harmony.

To commemorate the legend and bring good luck to the people, the Dai still celebrate the Water Sprinkling Festival. Water can be splashed gently or aggressively, and it is believed that the more one is splashed the happier one will be. Watching dragon boaters drench one another at an international competition, or triumphant hockey players soak themselves with champagne and beer after winning an important game, makes one realize just how important rituals still are even in a world as technological as the one we live in.

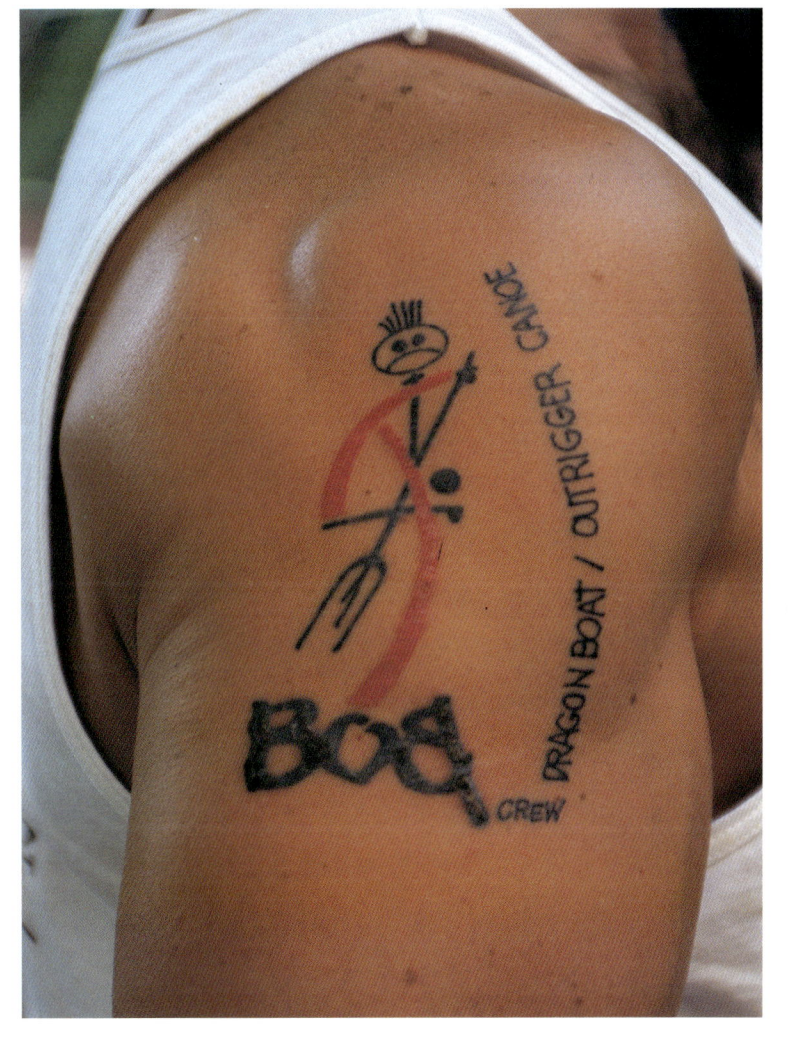

"Lately tattooing and body painting have become popular with some dragon boaters." Here a member of Vancouver's Team Bob proudly displays his decoration.

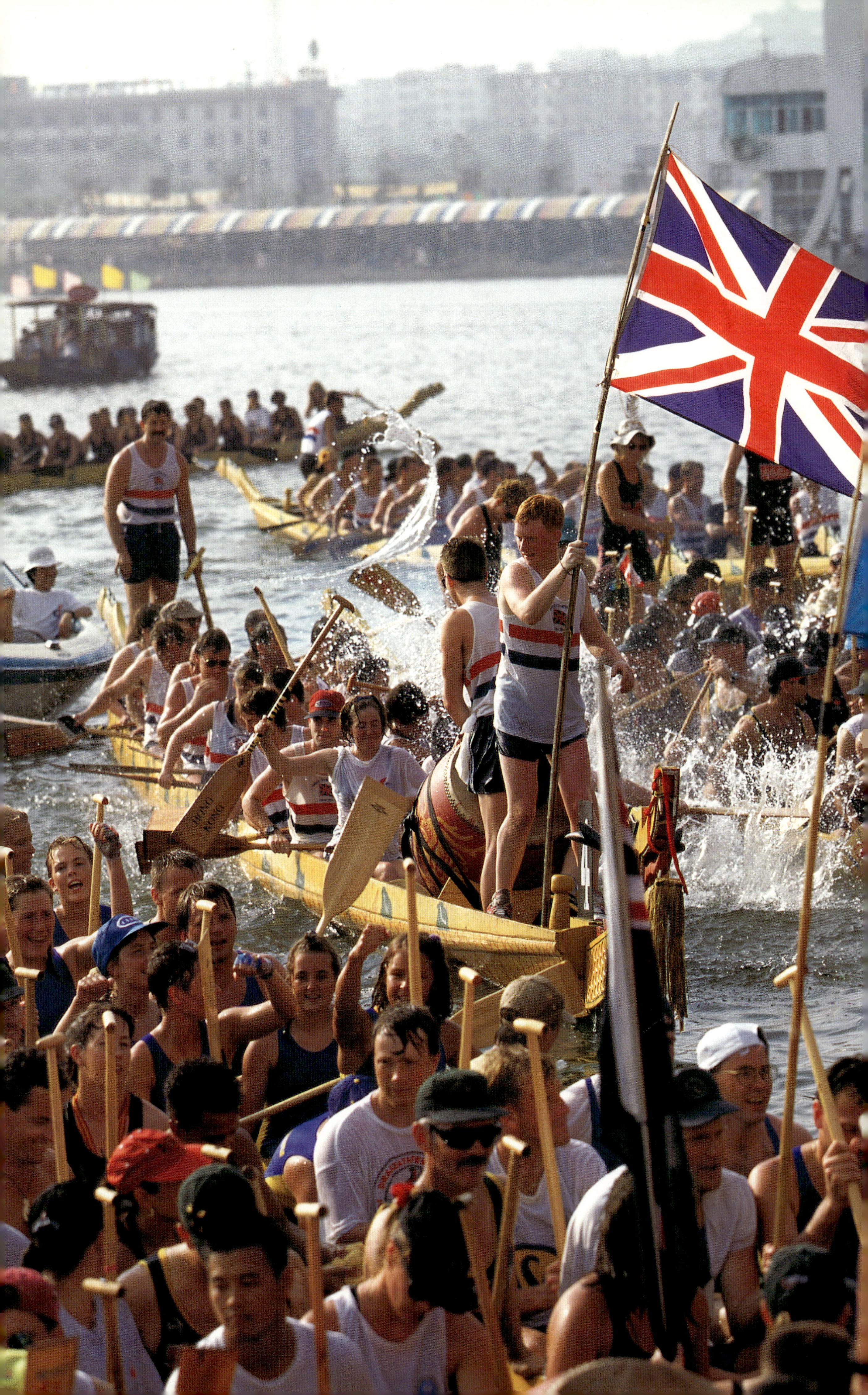
HONG KONG

4 Delighting the Senses

Festivals and Races Around the World

The morning rays have not yet hit the city skyline, but already groups of tai chi chuan practitioners have been up for nearly an hour. Thousands gather along the waterfront and wooded parklands of Hong Kong for what appears to be a slow-motion ballet requiring control and balance. Suddenly the buildings become a canvas of the sun's reflections, and color bleeds across tens of thousands of glass office windows. Bamboo stands, colorful flags, and huge barges are set up around the racecourse off Tsim Sha Tsui waterfront. The barges help to minimize the wake in Victoria Harbour, one of the busiest channels in the world, but this morning the surf is particularly rough. Waves come in hard against the dragon boats that are out practicing in the harbor, and with each hit the drummer ponders how long it will take to heave him and his teammates into the murky water.

The races present a picturesque spectacle. The long, narrow dragon-like boats with the dusky, half-naked rowers, the spray cast up by the glistening paddles, the rhythmic motion responding to gong and drum — these once seen are not soon forgotten.

— Lewis Hodous, Folkways in China

Hong Kong Dragon Boat Festival

The idea of balance is one that has been practiced in China for thousands of years. Today inhabitants of Hong Kong seek a delicate balance between old and new, between yin and yang, between a profitable past and an uncertain future. In a world of modern finance and commerce, age-old beliefs such as numerology, geomancy, and ancestor worship still play an important part in the lives of Hong Kong's 5.9 million people.

At the 1995 Hong Kong Dragon Boat Festival, paddlers must achieve their own delicate balance in what is certainly one of the toughest racecourses any of them will ever face. "There is always that feeling of the ground moving when you come off your boat in Hong

Teams from around the world unite at the awards presentation in Yueyang in 1995.

DRAGON BOATS: A CELEBRATION

Hong Kong is renowned for its neon signage.

Kong," comments Iain Fisher of Vancouver's False Creek men's team. Fisher, the team's stroke, is used to paddling in variable conditions from snow and rain to brilliant sunshine and balmy temperatures, but "paddling in this chop is an event in itself," he insists.

This is Fisher's fifth trip to Hong Kong, and when asked what keeps him coming back, he says, "This is the place you'll find the competition. All the best teams come here. Besides," he adds with a smile, "there is always the challenge of coming in first." Fisher and his teammates have nearly tasted gold on three occasions, and with a trio of sil-

DELIGHTING THE SENSES

vers in their closet, the team is back for another shot at gold.

Hong Kong held its first international event in 1976, thanks to one entry from Japan, and has since become the standard for races around the world. Today more than 40 international teams and 129 local teams participate in the Hong Kong festival.

Unofficially the races in Hong Kong have been known as the "world championships" of dragon boating. Now, thanks to the organization of the International Dragon Boat Federation (IDBF), a different city will hold the official world championships every second year. The first such event took place in June 1995 in Yueyang, China, the legendary birthplace of dragon boating.

In 1996 the races in Hong Kong will most likely be held on the Shing-Mun River in the New Territories, which means future races will no longer take place on the Tsim Sha Tsui waterfront. On June 14 and 15, 1997, Hong Kong will host the second IDBF World Championships. This will occur at a historical moment, since the event will take place two weeks before the return of the territory to the People's Republic of China.

For Iain Fisher's False Creek men's team, though, 1995 means placing seventh in the men's finals, with Indonesia taking top honors, China's veteran Shun De crew finishing second, and a Toronto team snatching third. But Fisher's team finally captures gold in a heart-stopping race in

An Australian dragon boat team (foreground) in the marshaling area at the Hong Kong races.

DRAGON BOATS: A CELEBRATION

The grandstands in Nanhu Stadium in Yueyang.

the International Mixed category, while the False Creek women's crew manages to outpull the competition from China to capture gold for the fifth time in seven trips to Hong Kong. No matter how much dragon boating develops in other countries in the next century, winning, or even just competing, in Hong Kong will always remain special.

Yueyang Dragon Boat Festival, China

Filing off buses, the dragon boat teams make their way through crowds of spectators located just outside the gates. Thousands of people from all over China's Hunan Province have lined up against a fence surrounding the site in hopes of catching a glimpse of some 20 international teams that have come to the First World Championship Dragon Boat Races in Yueyang. The stadium at Nanhu Lake, part of the larger Dongting Lake, can hold 5,000 spectators, and a staggering half-million people can find standing room around the sports facility.

Much has been done in preparation to welcome the world to Yueyang, including the construction of a new mechanized metal-and-fiberglass starting system that is unique to the sport. The dragon boats are backed into "floats," or air-filled fiberglass cubes, that are joined together with a metal frame to form a kind of "floating sidewalk." When that is accomplished, an official attaches brackets to the vessels' tails, which hold the boats in place. Then mechanized vises move in around the sides of the boats at the eighth seat and hold the craft stationary until they are released by a master switch.

The day before the festival there are spectacular opening ceremonies, beginning with a parade the Chinese call the Dragon God

DELIGHTING THE SENSES

Phoenix and dragon carvings decorate the exquisite Yueyang Tower.

Ceremony. Hundreds of performers, many with paddles, escort the sacred dragon head to the race site for the evening fireworks display. The "dragons of the air" have sent rain showers for the opening ceremonies, but this doesn't deter thousands of umbrellas making their way into Nanhu Stadium. It is unlikely that foreign visitors have ever seen so many umbrellas at one event!

White doves are then released high above the clouds, and colorful balloons emblazon the dark gray skies. Boats that are nearly 100 feet long carry 40 to 130 people as they circle the lake in a cultural display of costumes and choreography. Under large straw hats a group of paddlers dressed in black reenact the search for Qu Yuan's body. Slowly and rhythmically, they hit their long paddles against the water in exaggerated, sweeping motions, while other multicolored boats decorated

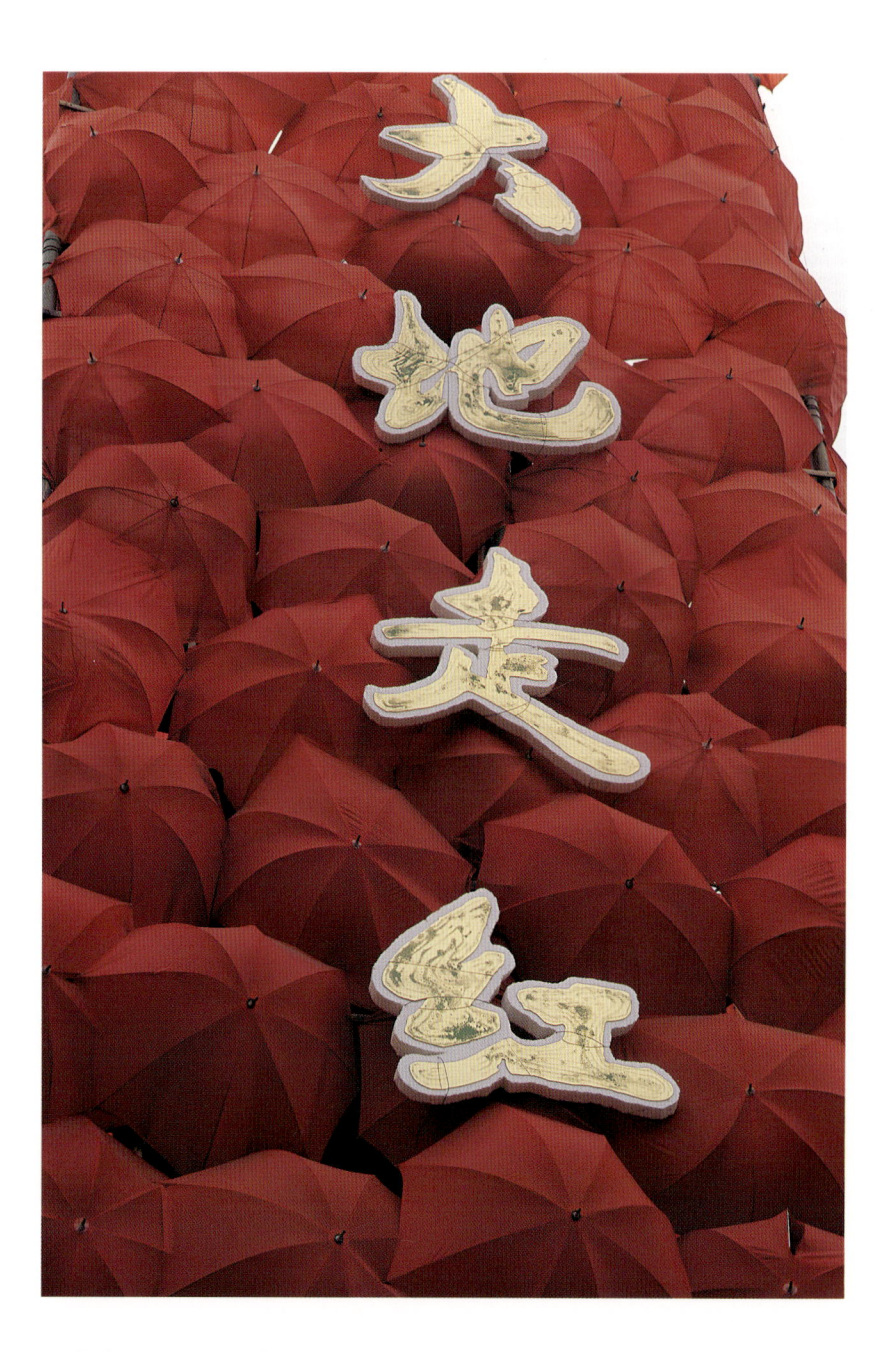

A canopy of umbrellas crowds the entrance to Yueyang's fairgrounds.

大地走红

with flags carry performing folk dancers, as well as musicians who play cymbals, gongs, drums, and horns.

Spectators, mostly from Yueyang and nearby villages, stand transfixed by the cultural display. Dragon boat culture has been a part of this area, the alleged birthplace of dragon boating, for more than 2,000 years. "Paddling past the crowd was amazing," says Jackie Webber of the False Creek women's team. "When we went past the Chinese people with our Canadian flag, the people waved, smiled, and really cheered us on. They threw red and gold lanterns into the water as gifts to us. I'll always remember that."

Besides a full complement of men's, women's, and mixed races, the Yueyang festival also features a "folk class" division that showcases the different boat cultures of China. There are ivory dragon boats made by the Dai Zu people of Yunnan Province, decorative craft from the Guyue district, canoes of the Miao Zu people, and flowery vessels from Guilin. These long boats are the true dragon boats, for the smaller boats used in international dragon boating were only developed in the past 20 years.

In the international races, Shun De, a team from Guangdong Province in China, tastes revenge in Yueyang for their defeats in Hong Kong as their teams snatch gold and bronze in all three divisions. Vancouver's False Creek women's team places second in both the women's and mixed categories; a men's team from Philadelphia grabs silver in the 1,000-meter competition; Indonesia, so successful in Hong Kong, settles for a silver and bronze; and teams from New Zealand, Sweden, and Germany place third in various categories.

And then it is all over, except for closing ceremonies that few festivals can even contemplate. Gigantic dragon barges with heads towering over the water join in the procession. Similar to modern-day parade floats, the barges are lavishly decorated with flowers and flags and hold dancers, musicians, and flag bearers who provide entertainment for the thousands of spectators lining the shores of Nanhu Lake. And, of course, all competitors are invited to join in the Yueyang-style "sail through" that fittingly marks a milestone in the evolution of a sport that continues to amaze. Nineteen ninety-six won't bring another world championship to Yueyang, but all of the competitors at this event know that dragon boating is alive and well in its birthplace.

Singapore International Dragon Boat Festival

"We are, we are ugly! U-G-L-Y, ugly! We are, we are False Creek! We are, we are ugly!" chant the two teams that hail from Vancouver.

"You're not wrong there, mate!" quips a member of the Australian team.

Laughter, which is heard all around, is magnified under the bridge where foreign competitors prepare for the "sail past" of Singapore's 1995 dragon boat festival. One by one the teams will be officially announced and welcomed by the crowd as they are called upon to paddle past thousands of spectators lining the shore. From each dragon boat, paddlers will return a wave, give a team cheer, or perhaps provide the audience with a choreographed display of paddling.

Gathered together on the water, teams vie for the only shade provided by the bridge overhead. As they are marshaled into their assigned

DRAGON BOATS: A CELEBRATION

positions, the noise under the bridge builds and teams let off steam for their first day of competition. An earth-shaking drum roll comes from the Malaysian team, whose drummer silences the crowd with an awesome display of talent. Next, the drummer from the False Creek men's team, a minister of the Squamish people, begins his prerace ritual and psych-out of the other teams. For years he has graced the front pages of international newspapers with his First Nations attire replete with feathered headdress. Then the Indonesian team takes over, and even the drummers from Malaysia and Canada stop drumming in appreciation of this "maestro." With five hard hits of the drum, the Indonesian finishes his solo and everyone on the bridge breaks into applause. They seem oblivious to the marshals who are there to keep some semblance of order, their megaphones drowned out by the crescendo under the bridge.

Singapore has been hosting dragon boat races in Marina Bay for more than 15 years. In 1987 the city-nation held its first international race, and three years later it staged its first world invitational dragon boat competition, attracting 17 teams from 15 countries. The races are held over two days, with 10 days of festival activities. In 1992 the festival added "baby" dragon boats to the event. Built for a 12-person team, these small boats are now used for the open women's race. The open men's division draws teams from all over the world with the lure of prize money totaling US $18,000 to the top three finishers.

The False Creek women's team in blistering action during a training session in Vancouver.

"Up, up, up!" cries the drummer, and the repeated word is music to the ears of all the dragon boat racers. If the race seems longer than usual, it is because the Singapore racecourse measures 700 meters, 60 meters longer than most courses found in the rest of the world. Three cheers are heard for the winners, who reciprocate in kind for everyone else. As the teams make their way back to the loading dock, applause breaks out along the shore in appreciation of a race well done. This semifinal has turned into a final for many of the teams . . . until next year, that is.

Thailand International Swan Boat Races

The sport of paddling long boats has been a part of Thailand's heritage for centuries. These long, majestic craft, known as swan boats, are quite different to paddle than Chinese dragon boats.

"The boats are very 'tender,'" says Adrian Lee of Vancouver's Canadian International Dragon Boat Festival. Lee, who is a dragon boat fanatic, took part in the 1990 Thailand festival when it was on the Chao Phraya River near the Rama IX Bridge in Bangkok. He describes the boats as being "similar to an outrigger canoe, but without the ama and more flaired at the sides." As a result, he says, the boats take a bit of getting used to in that they respond easily to movement within the boat.

"Another consideration is the paddles they use in Thailand," says Lee. "They don't have T-grip paddles, so it's an entirely different paddling technique." Maintaining the correct blade angle seems to be the most common challenge in using these paddles, for without the customary top-hand grip the shaft easily slides around in a paddler's hand.

"The paddles also have a longer blade," says Lee. "This kind of threw our team off for a while. It took a few runs for us to realize that we only had two-thirds of the paddle in the water."

Also unlike the dragon boats, which seat a drummer up high, swan boats use a coxswain who sits low in the boat. Without a drummer the cox must rely entirely on a loud voice to be heard above the noise of a race. Lee claims it took a while for the team he steered to get used to an entirely different way of paddling. "These aren't dragon boats," claims Lee. "You really have to go into the Thai races and forget everything you've learned about dragon boating and learn to paddle all over again." Because the paddles are both longer and heavier than a dragon boat paddle, Lee says that it takes a shorter, faster rate to get the boats up and moving.

Thailand held its first international festival in 1988. The date of the festival isn't fixed, nor is the location, although usually it is held in Bangkok. Thailand's Tourism Authority organizes the festival and has been sending teams to international competitions since 1985.

Onam Festival and Snake Boat Races, India

The man paddling in the unusually shaped long boat looks surprisingly relaxed as he reaches down for the water far below him. His feet are locked and his thighs are tightly wrapped around the boat's prow. He is as far up the vessel as he can possibly go, and his fellow paddlers, a staggering 150 of them, reach out in front with both hands grasping the shafts of their paddles.

Thousands of spectators line the seashore for the annual Onam Festival and Snake Boat Races, which take place throughout the state of Kerala. Located in the southwestern tip of India, the state is hugged by mountains to the east and the Arabian Sea to the west. Until recent times Kerala was wholly dependent on the spice trade, which dates back 3,000 years. Pepper, cardamom, cinnamon, mace, ginger, nutmeg, and turmeric are some of the spices that have made Kerala the spice capital of the world.

The Onam is the most popular festival in Kerala, a land where fes-

As many as 150 paddlers can crowd into one of India's elaborate snake boats during the state of Kerala's Onam Festival. Courtesy of the India Tourist Office, Toronto, Canada.

tivals abound. Taking place in August-September one week prior to the full moon, the celebration has many similarities to the sport of dragon boat racing, including the fact that its origins can be traced back to the ancient harvesting of crops.

The Onam's serpentlike boats, with sterns extending high over the water, are an imposing sight and are the highlight of the festival. One hundred and fifty men paddle the majestic boats, which are festooned with beautiful ornamental umbrellas and elaborately designed banners. Traditions such as the painting of homes, the decorating of courtyards with flowers, and the eating of sumptuous feasts are also features of the Onam, reflections, it is said, of an ancient belief that an ideal society of peace and plenty once existed in ancient Kerala.

Canadian International Dragon Boat Festival, Vancouver

Sonny Wong, the Canadian International Dragon Boat Festival's general manager, points to one of the reasons for this event's tremendous success when he says, "The festival celebrates the cultural diversity of all Canadians." Vancouver was introduced to the sport in 1986 when, in accordance with Expo 86's theme of transportation and communication, six teak boats were sent as a gift from Hong Kong.

Located in front of Concord Pacific Place, the racecourse extends 640 meters from the dome of the Science World to the Cambie Street Bridge. The festival's organizing committee encourages participation at every level, which means there are a variety of racing classes and categories to accommodate different skill levels.

All participating teams at this festival, which usually takes place in mid-June, are guaranteed three races over two days of competition. Ed Ng, one of the members of the organizing committee, says that teams are self-seeded as part of an honors system that is dependent on race experience and number of practices prior to the festival. The 1995 races didn't include a men's division, partially due to an overwhelming interest in the mixed category. Nearly 80 teams competed in this division, with more than 100 teams taking part in the three-day festival as a whole.

Thousands of participants and spectators gather under the glass awning of the Plaza of Nations for the opening ceremonies. The Lieutenant Governor's Paddle, carved by artist William Koochin, is passed among festival participants as a ritual gesture of unity and as a signal that the festival has officially begun. Numerous food and beverage booths surround the plaza, which is packed with people enjoying music and

DRAGON BOATS: A CELEBRATION

Closing ceremonies at the 1995 Canadian International Dragon Boat Festival in Vancouver.

dancing on the center stage. Inside the Discovery Theatre the talents of artists from around the Pacific Rim are displayed.

In and around the marshaling area racers warm up, put on life jackets, and sort through hundreds of paddles to find the right one. Like most festivals, there is little opportunity for a warm-up in the boat, which must be paddled directly to the race start. Both traditional teak boats and fiberglass vessels are used in the Vancouver races.

Lanes are divided by race buoys, and boats are positioned between ropes located behind and in front of the craft. All boats are brought up slowly to the front rope, and when the official is happy with the lineup, the starter gives the command and the boats are off. On the last evening of the festival, after the presentation of awards, competitors are invited to participate in music, dancing, and, of course, T-shirt trading, which has become an event in itself.

The festival is never at a loss for new and imaginative team names such as Dragon Hags, Just Dragon Along, Either Or, Prelude to Pain, Blazing Paddles, and Dragon Our Butts. Nineteen ninety-five was also the inaugural contest for best T-shirt design, a popular event among the festival's many artist-paddlers.

Every year the Canadian International Dragon Boat Festival introduces thousands of new people to the sport of dragon boating. In 1995

DELIGHTING THE SENSES

The Lieutenant Governor's Paddle, carved by William Koochin, is passed around at the opening ceremonies of Vancouver's dragon boat festival.

more than 100,000 people took in the sights, sounds, and culinary delights of the festival, and in 1996 Vancouver will host the IDBF's First World Club Crew Championships at False Creek, an occasion that will no doubt attract even greater crowds and more teams from around the globe.

Victoria Dragon Boat Festival, Canada

"All right, team! Line up, please. Photo opportunity!" yells the coach.

"Which way do we look?" jests one of the paddlers from a team that calls itself the Eye of the Dragon. The name is appropriate for this Vancouver team, which relies on *feeling* rather than *seeing* the timing of the boat.

79

DRAGON BOATS: A CELEBRATION

"Almost half the team is visually impaired," explains their coach, Kim Graham. In describing the skill level of the team, she says, "We have every caliber of paddler, from those who just rolled off the couch to those who are very physically active. The great thing about taking up dragon boating is that it's really quite an easy sport to do."

Members of the Eye of the Dragon have come from Vancouver to take part in the first annual Victoria Dragon Boat Festival, presented by the Victoria Chinese Commerce Association. Twenty-one teams are competing in this inaugural 1995 festival, and race organizers can easily boast about having one of the most picturesque dragon boat sites in the world.

Located in Victoria's Inner Harbour, the races offer an excellent view for spectators and athletes alike, who can line up on the three sides that surround the finish line. Only a one-day regatta with four lanes of boats per race, this new dragon boat festival will no doubt increase in popularity in the years to come if the success of the festival in Vancouver, Victoria's larger counterpart across the Strait of Georgia, is any indication.

Victoria's jewel-like Inner Harbour makes an excellent site for the city's new dragon boat festival.

80

Alberta Dragon Boat Race Festival, Canada

"Roosta-sha, roosta-sha, roosta-sha-sha. Thumbs up! Wrists together! Elbows out! Butts out! Tongues out!" a Vancouver dragon boat team called Bob chants in a large circle in Calgary, Alberta, before heading out to the marshaling area. If the Maori *haka* can intimidate, the "Roosta-sha" does the exact opposite. The many teams and spectators taking in this prerace spectacle laugh uproariously and applaud.

Since its first appearance in 1992, Calgary's festival, which is held over the long weekend in August, has become one of the largest such affairs in Canada's West, with more than 30,000 spectators and 1,500 racers making the 1995 version a smashing success. The 650-meter course is located at the Glenmore Reservoir, the source of the city's water supply and home to both the Calgary Canoe Club and Calgary Rowing Club. The festival's six fiberglass dragon boats hold 18 paddlers, two fewer than the standard vessel.

Kamini Jain, a competitive kayaker and coach from Calgary, says the festival has a "beautiful site with a clear view of the Rocky Mountains, and the racecourse is also good from a spectator's point of view since you can see all the way down it without any problem." Jain also relates that although the festival hasn't hosted foreign teams yet, "the sport is growing really fast and the racers have become highly competitive." She also points out that "Visiting Calgary opens up other travel possibilities in the Rockies. Racers can turn their trip into a natural wilderness adventure, too. Besides," she says with a laugh, "we have great parties."

National Capital Dragon Boat Race Festival, Ottawa, Canada

"Whiskers" is the word paddler Darren Johnson uses to describe how much his team lost by in the grand final of Ottawa's 1995 National Capital Dragon Boat Race Festival. Competing in the men's division, this mixed crew from Vancouver created a stir by winning the 100-meter sprint. Later, however, Johnson's team was narrowly beaten by the Ottawa Rideau Canoe Club on the 640-meter course. Third place was taken by the Marathon Voyageurs, a team of long-distance canoe racers from Ontario and Quebec.

Ottawa's dragon boat festival, which was first held at the Rideau Canoe Club on Mooney's Bay in 1994, allows racers to test their strengths in two different distances, as well as take in the performing arts and a food fair. Organized by the Hong Kong Canada Business Association, the festival uses traditional teak dragon boats and supplies

No matter what festival dragon boaters participate in, camaraderie among competitors is always foremost, as demonstrated by these racers in Hong Kong.

teams with life jackets and paddles for a full day of events. Thirty-two teams and 5,000 spectators took part in the 1995 festival, which is now an annual event usually held in August.

Toronto International Dragon Boat Race Festival, Canada

The lineup for Toronto's Centre Island pulses with expectation as teams and spectators make their way onto the ferry. Corporate teams, which stand out with their matching uniforms and paddles, now place the Toronto International Dragon Boat Race Festival on their social calendar, inviting family and friends to take part in the June weekend festival. In fact, more than 100 teams and 120,000 people will make the ten-minute journey over to Centre Island by the time the festival closes.

The cluster of islands in Toronto's Lake Ontario harbor boast a terrific view of the city's skyline and serve as a lush green refuge for those seeking escape from urban sprawl. "I've never been to a festival site as tranquil and pastoral as Toronto's," claims one competitor as he steps off the ferry. He and his team quickly make their way over to one of the islands to set up tents, drop off coolers filled with food for barbecues, and prepare for the day's events. There is definitely something of a holiday feel in the balmy air.

Since hosting its first festival in 1989, Toronto has witnessed a dramatic rise in dragon boat enthusiasm. There are now a number of races in Metropolitan Toronto, and it looks as if many other southern Ontario cities might soon have their own festivals, joining Hamilton, Ottawa, and London.

DELIGHTING THE SENSES

Colorful and elaborate dragon boat figureheads are always one of the highlights of any festival.

Sharifa Khan, president of the Toronto Chinese Business Association and the festival's development director, says, "Last year's festival surpassed all expectations in terms of attendance and participation. We had a 20 percent increase in attendance, and the festival drew a record 104 teams, up from 72 in 1994. This year we drew teams from as far away as Britain, Italy, and the Philippines." The event reached a milestone in 1993 when it went "international," and since then it has gone from strength to strength, undoubtedly ensuring its future success.

The two-day festival, which usually takes place in mid-June, uses six traditional teak dragon boats over a 640-meter course. The site on Centre Island is an ideal location since its waters are protected from high winds and passing boats. Of course, there is more to Toronto's festival than just racing, for this is a festival in the true sense of the word. Non-stop multicultural entertainment, featuring a wide variety of folk dancers and singers, cultural displays, and a culinary fair give the Toronto festival its international air and flair.

The festival draws top-caliber teams in men's, women's, and mixed categories, with the winners of the finals representing Toronto at the Hong Kong Dragon Boat Festival, while the victors in the Community Race are flown to the Canadian International Dragon Boat Festival in Vancouver. Youth and high school divisions are also featured in this festival, giving just about everybody a chance to experience the sport.

Another three-day dragon boat festival is held in conjunction with the CHIN-Radio International Picnic on the waterfront at Ontario Place. The races themselves are held on July 1, and the festival offers paddlers a wide variety of entertainment. Inner-city challenge races for kids between the Parks and Recreation Centres of Toronto and Hamilton, usually staged in June, are yet another manifestation of how popular dragon boating has become in Ontario's capital.

Khan explains that the main Toronto festival in mid-June "assists a number of other festivals in southern Ontario, including those in Ottawa and London. And Toronto will also be instrumental in the organization of the Montreal Dragon Boat Festival, which will be launched in 1996." Clearly dragon boating has really taken hold in central Canada.

Pacific Northwest International Dragon Cup, Seattle, Washington

As the team known as Mountain Home Canoe from Portland, Oregon, crosses the finish line, paddles are raised high in the familiar sign of victory. Mountain Home Canoe has just edged out its rival from Vancouver, a team called Mackenzie. "It was great to win this," says Tom Meurlott of Mountain Home Canoe. Then he adds, "Team Mackenzie beat us in Vancouver a few weeks ago, so this was a good win for us here."

A friendly rivalry is developing among the paddling teams of the Pacific Northwest. In late July, 26 teams from Washington, Oregon, and British Columbia have come together on Lake Washington for the Second Annual Pacific Northwest International Dragon Cup. The 500-meter racecourse, located at the Stanley Sayres Boat Pits, provides spectators and athletes with an excellent vantage point, with the finish line just a stone's throw from the shore. And, besides the excite-

The taste of victory at Seattle's Pacific Northwest International Dragon Cup in 1995.

ment of the races, participants and spectators can take in a day of cultural entertainment and culinary delights.

Tom Meurlott says he was quite taken by the hospitality at the Seattle festival: "It was a small but really friendly festival. The people there were really nice. They came up and thanked our team for coming up. You don't get that at the larger festivals."

Portland Rose Festival Dragon Boat Races, Oregon

Wedged into the space on top of the dragon head, the flag catcher recoils like a spring, extends her arm way out, and in a last-ditch effort lunges forward to grasp the flag from the post. The boat she is in finishes a split second behind the neighboring team, but because the flag catcher has grabbed the flag first, her team is the overall winner of the heat. Needless to say, her team is ecstatic with the result, and as the "heroine" dismounts from her perch, she disappears into a flurry of hugs and slaps on the back.

Such is the racing format of the Portland dragon boat races. Placing is determined not by who crosses the finish line first, but the team

Flag catcher practicing at the Portland Rose Festival Dragon Boat Races in 1995.

first able to snatch a flag from a post at the end of the lane. Moments before the boat reaches the finish line, an assigned flag catcher must carefully position herself on top of a massive dragon head to grab a flag at the finish line.

The Portland boats, which come from Taiwan, are larger than their teak dragon boat cousins from Hong Kong and are affectionately referred to as "barges" by most of the paddling community. The paddles used in the present-day festival are a far cry from the gigantic ones used in Portland's earlier events. The enormous red paddles were quite a sight when seen for the first time. Fortunately for competitors, the old paddles were showing signs of wear and were eventually replaced by lighter versions.

The technique for paddling Portland's huge vessels is somewhat different than that used to move the lighter teak and fiberglass dragon boats. According to many of the crews, "A great deal of abdominal strength is required. It feels as if you're doing a start for the duration of the race."

The Portland festival began in 1989 when the city forged ties with Kaohsiung, Taiwan, one of the 10 largest ports in the world. The event is sponsored by the Portland-Kaohsiung Sister City Association and is held in conjuction with the Portland Rose Festival, which usually takes place in early June. The 10-day combined festival attracts thousands of people to the fairgrounds on the Willamette River, and more than 90 teams compete during two days of racing. This event has become a popular festival with racers from the Greater Vancouver area, who use the occasion to prepare for their own festival.

Interestingly enough, the first dragon boat competition on the North American continent may have occurred in Portland in 1836 when it was reported that races were held on the Festival of the Double Fifth and prizes were awarded in the form of gold and dresses. These prizes were fastened to the winning post (not unlike the flags in today's races), which was stuck in the Willamette's mud. The object was to reach the post first and secure the prize. Naturally a great deal of gambling on the outcome took place among spectators. However, the city of Boston would no doubt dispute Portland's claim, since its dragon boat races date back to 1979 and are most likely the earliest continuous races in North America.

U.S.A. International Dragon Boat Festival, Burlington, Iowa

FRIENDSHIP THROUGH PADDLING has become the motto of the American Dragon Boat Association (ADBA) in promoting the U.S.A. International Dragon Boat Festival. "In addition to the international races that were held in Burlington, Iowa, in September 1995," says Carlos Capdevila, paddler and co-chairman of the festival, "we also hold our own local races, which have proven to be extremely popular in the Midwest. The U.S.A. festival actually rotates between the Iowa cities of Burlington, Dubuque, and Cedar Rapids." Capdevila, who also steers a team that calls itself the Budragons, adds, "In September 1996 the festival will be held in Dubuque."

There is plenty of other racing in the Midwest, too, says Capdevila, in such communities along the Mississippi River as Iowa City, St. Charles, Red Wing, Stillwater, and about 30 other places. "We circulate 14 boats that are used almost every week, which makes the Midwest an attractive destination for teams looking for a lot of paddling. The main difference between our races, where we use traditional Taiwanese boats, is that while the Hong Kong-style dragon boat races are more conducive to the 'committed athlete,' the Taiwanese style of

T-shirts are always a hot item for avid collectors at dragon boat races around the world.

dragon boating is easier to do, which means our festival and races are more attractive to recreational paddlers."

Warming to his topic, Capdevila notes, "We have a novice division [30 teams this year], and the city of Burlington can boast the first dragon boat festival for high school students only. In 1996 our city is hoping to participate in an exchange program with high school students from Toronto, Canada, which will certainly add an international component to the racing and an exciting opportunity for the students."

The Burlington races are quite different from those in Hong Kong. The boats used in the American city are replicas of Taiwanese dragon boats that weigh nearly a ton. The finely crafted vessels, resplendent with enormous dragon heads and tails, are the highlight of a festival that retains a great deal of the sport's Chinese character.

The event in Burlington was launched by a small group of Optimist Club members in 1988 and takes place on the banks of the Mississippi at Seven Ponds Park. There were only a dozen teams that first year, a modest number for a festival that is currently the largest in the Midwest. Today around a quarter of a million people take in the numerous races and festivals that grace the banks of the Mississippi from Minnesota to Louisiana through much of the year, proving once again how adaptable dragon boating is and how far it has come in the past 2,000 years.

Hong Kong Dragon Boat Festival in New York

In the U.S. Midwest the American Dragon Boat Association holds sway, but in the east the United States Dragon Boat Association (USDBA) is the primary organizer of dragon boating. Operating out of Drexel Hall, Pennsylvania, this group promotes the sport in Washington, D.C., Boston, Baltimore, and Philadelphia. However, the biggest festival on the East Coast is in the Big Apple, where it is officially called the Hong Kong Dragon Boat Festival in New York. Not surprisingly, there is much in common between these two cultural capitals with their towering skylines, international banking, and renowned shopping that attract millions of visitors and business travelers year-round. In fact, the main goal of the New York festival, according to organizers, is to "foster friendship and understanding between these two cities."

David Tsui, director of the Hong Kong Economic and Trade Office in New York, says his agency stages the festival in conjunction with the Hong Kong Association of New York. He claims that his festival is "an Oriental celebration blended with a bit of Western flavor. In a sense, it's an opportunity for East to meet West and make something truly wonderful. We have all kinds of teams from various corporations that use the festival as an opportunity to build staff morale. These people have a unique opportunity to practice together and get to know people in their respective organizations."

The New York festival has come a long way since its beginning in 1991. The races drew only 10 teams that first year, while today more than 50 teams compete on the 500-meter course at Flushing Meadows Corona Park. The festival is held over two weekends in August, with the winning teams of the first event competing against several teams from across the country at the championship races the following Sunday. The winners of this race are awarded a team trip to the dragon boat festival in Hong Kong the following year.

New York's festival uses traditional teak dragon boats from Hong Kong, and in addition to the 500-meter racecourse, paddlers can test their sprint and endurance capacities on new 250-meter and 1,000-meter courses.

*Teak dragon boats nestle together before a race: a moment of
tranquillity prior to the clamor of competition.*

Besides the excitement of the races at Flushing Meadows, there are over 30 booths in Hong Kong Village where racers and spectators can watch artisans practice Chinese calligraphy, traditional ink brush painting, and paper cutting. Also included in the festival lineup are a variety of performing arts, a food fair, and, of course, plenty of racing. To cap it all off, the festival wraps up with a banquet in New York's Chinatown. In 1995 the dinner was attended by a thousand people. Now that's a feast!

London International Dragon Boat Races, England

Britain's capital is world-renowned for its double-decker buses, but the vehicle received even more publicity when it was recently pulled by a local dragon boat team. Jean Price of the Hartlepool Powermen, which despite its name actually includes a few women, recaps the event: "It started with a local TV program called *You Bet*. The idea of the program is to have different personalities try to do silly things so that people can bet whether it can be done or not. Our bet was to pull a double-decker 50 yards or so in a predetermined time." When asked if they succeeded, Price replies, "It was very difficult and we couldn't get the bus to move at first." However, after a few practice starts, the team eventually got the bus up and running, demonstrating once again the power of dragon boating!

Jim McArthur and Peter Zubick, paddler/coaches with Vancouver's Lotus Eaters, have had the opportunity to coach the Hartlepool Powermen. Zubick says, "It's quite an active league all over Britain. Every club owns one or two boats and they can race just about every weekend if they want." Zubick feels that this really adds to the excitement of racing in the country, for just like rugby leagues, dragon boat teams can combine a series of races and tour the United Kingdom.

McArthur, on his part, points out that British races are very intimate affairs. Everyone knows everyone else and the camaraderie among teams is evident right from the start. He says that although the British teams are highly competitive, the races are "stereotypically British." When asked exactly what he means by that comment, he answers, "Everyone was so congenial, so civilized." McArthur recalls one training session when between practices the team paddled down to the end of the harbor, hopped into the local pub for a quick pint, and then returned to resume training.

London has held annual dragon boat races since 1989, either on the Serpentine Lake in Hyde Park or at the London Docklands on the

Thames River. For the first four years of competition the races were staged in conjunction with the national finals of the British Dragon Boat Racing Association's Charity Challenge. This competition has raised nearly one million pounds for charity over the past seven years.

London's dragon boat festival is primarily aimed at European crews and forms part of the Eurocup competition organized by the European Dragon Boat Federation (EDBF). As such, it has attracted entries from Germany, Sweden, Norway, Italy, Switzerland, and Holland, in addition to crews from Canada and the Philippines. The number of competitors averages between 600 to 800, representing 30 to 40 different crews.

The number of spectators varies according to the weather, but crowds of 50,000 per day are not unusual at this event, which is held in mid-September. In 1995, with the support of the Hong Kong Government Office in London, the dragon boat festival became part of a Hong Kong Chinese Festival, complete with cultural displays and traditional food booths on the Serpentine Lake. Entry to the festival is free, and it is intended that the London Hong Kong Chinese Festival and Dragon Boat Races will become an annual event in the calendar of attractions of Britain's capital.

Rome Dragon Boat Festival, Italy

Castel Gandolfo is a small town overlooking Lake Albano on the outskirts of Rome. It gets its name from the Genoese family of the Gandolfi dukes who, in the 12th century, built a castle on the lakeshore. In recent times the town's main claims to fame are that it serves as the pope's summer residence and that it was used as a site for the rowing championships in the 1960 Olympic Games. Signs and gates sporting the Olympic symbol still line the main street near the waterfront.

In 1995 Castel Gandolfo could claim something else: it was the site of Rome's first dragon boat festival. Four fiberglass boats were used in each heat, and unlike the case with most festivals, many teams brought their own boats.

Sarina McKenzie, who hails from Vancouver, joined up with a mixed team from Canada to make the journey to Italy and found freshwater paddling a surprise. "I was a bit overwhelmed paddling in fresh water for the first time," states McKenzie. "The white water coming off the front of the boat was quite challenging that first day. Stroking the boat was like punching a wall with every recovery of the paddle."

Italy is a relative newcomer to dragon boating. Here one of the country's mixed teams competes in Yueyang.

Another challenge for her team was finding a comfortable seating position. For without the usual center and foot pieces to brace against, there was plenty of shifting around at first. McKenzie notes that some of the equipment, such as the festival paddles, came from the races in Yueyang, while the drums on the dragon boats came from Hong Kong.

There were three divisions at the Castel Gandolfo event: mixed, open, and women's. Race distances included 250-meter and 500-meter sprints, and the festival closed with a dinner and dance and a different kind of "boat racing" – a drinking game. This event was comprised of 10-person teams and was almost as popular as the dragon boat races themselves. McKenzie claims that her team came up with two third- and one fourth-place finishes in the dragon boat festival. As for the drinking game, she smiles and says, "We won overwhelmingly!"

Florence International Dragon Boat Regatta, Italy

Under the Ponte Vecchio Bridge crowds of onlookers take a break from their shopping to catch a glimpse of the First International Dragon Boat Regatta in Florence in the fall of 1995. Red and white rosebushes line the banks of the Arno River, which is shared by rowers from Societa Canottieri Di Firenze, a club that was established in the early 1900s. To paddle in this festival, a team from Canada has joined forces with Tuscia and Drago Volance, two dragon boat teams from Italy.

"The races in Florence were really exciting," claims Dario Baldasso, a paddler/coach of Italian descent from Vancouver. He found the races in Italy a wonderful opportunity to explore his heritage. "My parents were born in Selva Del Montello on the outskirts of Venice," says Baldasso, who took a bit of extra time off to visit his parents' hometown. "The racing was very challenging, especially trying to get three teams that have never paddled together to merge as one over such a short time."

"The Italians who paddled with us didn't understand much English," adds teammate Sarina McKenzie, "but fortunately our coach was able to make the calls in Italian. We weren't certain what he was saying exactly, but we've raced often enough together to know the order of the calls. Having the commands shouted out in another language didn't affect our performance and it really helped out the Italians."

Prior to the final race, the open men's 250 meters, there was a delay that caused the Italian-Canadian team to seek shade under the bridge. "Normally," says McKenzie, "I'm pretty focused, but we had so much time before the race that I was able to actually absorb the unfamiliar surroundings. I had time to ponder the fact that here I was in Florence, sitting on the Arno River. That was quite exciting for me at the time."

Lambton Harbour Dragon Boat Festival, Wellington, New Zealand

To witness a Maori *haka* prior to a dragon boat race is to see the whole body speak of canoe culture. In precolonial times the Maori war canoe was a vital part of this indigenous people's civilization. Recently there has been a rebirth of canoe culture in New Zealand, and with the introduction of dragon boating in the 1980s, New Zealanders of all backgrounds have taken to the sport as if it were their own, even to the point of renaming the dragon boats *waka,* Maori for "war canoe."

New Zealanders begin dragon boat training in November and kick off their season with a couple of warm-up races such as the South Waikato and Tangaroa Regattas. Races are held every weekend throughout the country from the end of January through to the middle of March, and festivals now take place in Wellington, Auckland, Christchurch, and Dunedin, as well as numerous smaller towns around the country.

For six months of the year Wellington's harbor is transformed into training grounds for some 1,500 paddlers as they prepare for upcoming races. The Wellington festival has hosted dragon boating since 1987, and its 1995 version featured more than 100 crews watched by 50,000 spectators in Lambton Harbour.

At 320 meters the festival's racecourse is shorter than those found in Hong Kong or Vancouver, and race starts are also done a little differently. Here a rope is held taut above the heads of the drummers, who reach up to grab it when a one-minute call is announced and the starter has lined up all the boats. Then the starter shouts, "Paddles ready!" and a few seconds after that, a gunshot signals the start.

Now in its ninth year of dragon boating, Wellington hosts the New Zealand Nationals in 1996, and the city has been awarded the IDBF's International Club Crew Dragon Boat Championships for 1998. The kiwis hope to draw more than 35 international teams for the Club Crew Championships, and rumor has it that Wellington boasts one of the best dragon boat closing parties in the world!

Auckland's festival usually takes place over a weekend in February and attracts more than 40,000 people to the venue at Princess Wharf. The festival opens with very short 50-meter sprints, with 300-meter races held on Saturday and Sunday.

DRAGON BOATS: A CELEBRATION

Members of one of New Zealand's numerous dragon boat teams perform a ceremonial haka *at the Hong Kong Dragon Boat Festival.*

Melbourne Dragon Boat Festival, Australia

Like New Zealanders, Australians are quite taken with dragon boating, which they have embraced as their own since the early 1980s. Races and festivals are held in Adelaide, Brisbane, Canberra, Perth, Cairns, and many other communities from the beginning of February to early April, but the two biggest events, naturally, occur in Melbourne and Sydney.

The Victoria Dragon Boat Association holds an exciting one-day festival on Melbourne's Yarra River. Nineteen ninety-six will be the 13th year Melbourne has staged the event and the eighth year it has showcased international competition. The races draw as many as 40 teams to compete on a 500-meter racecourse, and the festival maintains the original aim of the Victoria Dragon Boat Association, which is "to foster greater understanding and appreciation of Chinese culture and tradition by broad community participation."

Most Melbourne teams begin their training in December and

continue practicing until the festival begins in March. Like many international dragon boat events, Melbourne's festival waives international registration fees and offers low-cost accommodation for visiting foreign teams.

Sydney Dragon Boat Festival, Australia

"Sydney's dragon boat festival has a unique racecourse," says Trevor Brown, a 12-year veteran paddler from that city, "because it's in Darling Harbour. Spectators can line up on three sides to watch the race, which begins in the harbor and passes under a bridge. Around 300,000 spectators and up to 100 teams make our festival one of Australia's big annual attractions."

Brown says the Sydney course is 500 meters and that the festival takes place in the city's Chinatown between mid-March and early April. One of the things he loves most about the sport is that it has allowed him to compete in places like China, Singapore, Hong Kong, and Penang. In 1996 he is looking forward to visiting Vancouver for the World Mixed Crew Championships.

An enthusiastic Australian crew initiates the first splashing at the awards ceremony of the Hong Kong races.

WHY HAS DRAGON BOATING made such a successful leap into a whole range of diverse cultures, from Italy and Sweden to New Zealand and Canada? Australia's prime minister, P. J. Keating, has said that dragon boating presents "an opportunity to continue to break down barriers of ignorance and prejudice and to promote tolerance and acceptance of difference." But he has also noted that dragon boating is "an exciting and colorful sport which is exhilarating to both participant and spectator alike." Keating's comments appear to describe an excellent combination that should ensure even greater success for dragon boating as the world marches into the next millennium.

Yueyang and the Buddha's Laughter

"You are young. This is how you pronounce the name of our city Yueyang," explains interpreter Xie Xue. "If you visit Yueyang, you will become younger," she adds, smiling. "There are nearly 63 million people in our province of Hunan. Chairman Mao Zedong was born close to Yueyang."

Xie Xue, or "Sharon," as she prefers to call herself in English, has been a most congenial hostess to all the dragon boat paddlers and media from Vancouver. We are here for the first world championships sanctioned by the International Dragon Boat Federation. Yueyang, the site of the races, is on the northeast shore of Dongting Lake, just south of the fabled Yangzi River.

For the next week Sharon will be up before 5:00 a.m. and to bed after midnight, playing volunteer tour guide for her foreign guests, all the while studying for an English teaching position in Yueyang. Her perpetual smile makes her appear to have an inexhaustible supply of energy. For our first outing she has taken us to the great Yueyang Tower, one of four such structures in China.

"Yueyang Tower is one of the best known towers in China," claims Sharon proudly, as if she had had a hand in building it. "It was originally built in 212 AD and was later rebuilt in the Tang style in the late 1800s. The tower has had different names over the centuries, but it has been called the Yueyang Tower ever since Li Bai, the mid-Tang dynasty poet, wrote a famous poem about it."

This three-story structure, we read in our guidebooks, stands more than 65 feet high and was built without crossbeams or nails. There are three pavilions at the site: the Pavilion of Magic Plums, which is named after the plum-shaped stones inside the building; the Pavilion in Memory of Du Fu, a poet who died in poverty; and the Three Drunks Pavilion, which is dedicated to one of the eight Taoist genii, Lu Tungpin, who was credited with preserving the tower and who reportedly was found drunk on the premises three times. During the Tang dynasty, this pavilion became a meeting place for famous Chinese writers.

"Yueyang is the place where the first dragon boat races were held more than 2,000 years ago," Sharon tells us after we leave the tower. "Tomorrow we will go to the Miluo River where the poet Qu Yuan committed suicide in 278 BC."

The next day our bus trip to the Miluo requires an interpreter, a guide, and a driver. The river is a three-hour journey from Yueyang through territory seeemingly devoid of signs; even our guide gets lost once along the way. By 5:30 a.m. there is already a continuous stream of cyclists navigating the main roads leading out of town, many of them loaded down with all kinds of merchandise for sale. It is not until the outskirts of the city that the swarms of cyclists dwindle to half a dozen every few miles.

Red-brick homes dot the rich green foothills in marked contrast to the city's endless tiers of gray homes stacked against an even grayer landscape. The bus is on a tight schedule, and the driver, like most of his colleagues here, follows no rules of the road and looks as if nothing will stop him. Then, suddenly, a small hen scoots out in front of the bus and we come to a screeching halt.

The moment the hen is out of harm's way, the driver once more begins his headlong flight down the paved road, which soon turns to gravel and finally to a deep red clay path that gradually becomes twisted and rutted. And, as tea and rice fields, grazing water buffalo, and children playing in streams flash by, we all wince at the thought of lost photo opportunities.

The bus arrives at Quzi Temple, located on Mount Yusi on the lower Miluo River. The province of Hunan has hundreds of such shrines commemorating Qu Yuan. A new temple, named after one of his poems, "Asking Heaven Altar," is under construction only 500 yards away. The Quzi Temple was originally built during the Han dynasty, then renovated during the Jin dynasty nearly 1,600 years ago. This temple is very special, for it holds the famous dragon head that is used in the Yueyang dragon boat festival's opening ceremonies.

The festival in Yueyang takes place over a 15-day period. Legend claims that Qu Yuan's body was discovered 10 days after he drowned, hence tradition dictates five days for the festival and 10 days of ceremony and celebration. Ten days prior to the festival, the temple's magnificent dragon head is taken down from its place of worship and moved to the shores of the Miluo. A special ceremony is held, followed by singing and dancing, and then the head is transported to the race site on Nanhu Lake where more ceremonies take place.

Many myths and legends surround the death of Qu Yuan. One of the gorier ones claims that when his body was discovered his head was found next to him, bitten off at the neck by fish. Qu Yuan's daughter supposedly cast the head in gold and buried her father in the mountains near Miluo City. To protect the great poet's grave, an additional 11 tombs were erected along the river in an attempt to mislead graverobbers.

The Quzi Temple is filled with photographs, scrolls, tablets, and paintings. Many of the scrolls and tablets are considered sacred to the Chinese. Black-and-white photographs of dragon boat races from the 1920s, a photograph of Mao Zedong (who, when young, strongly identified with the self-sacrificing Qu Yuan) visiting the temple, and paintings of Qu Yuan and his poems hang in individual black frames in rooms at the back of the place of worship. "This is the black scroll," comments Sharon reverently as we file past the treasure hoard. "It was carved in the Qing dynasty, but it has been covered up for many years. It was just recently uncovered in 1980."

The temple has managed to survive centuries of war and revolution and has apparently changed very little over the years. Although there is a gift store here selling plastic statues of Qu Yuan and English translations of his poetry, the area receives few foreign visitors despite its obvious tourist potential. Unfortunately the athletes back in Yueyang have a demanding race schedule, so few, if any, will be able to pay a visit to this enchanting site.

Leaving the temple, our bus makes a small detour to visit the shores of the Miluo. It is peaceful here, a welcome respite from the unceasing honking of car horns and general hustle and bustle of the city. Without trying very hard one can imagine Qu Yuan himself sitting here some 2,000 years ago contemplating life and its disappointments.

As we head back to Yueyang, Sharon tells us that we must see Junshan Island. "It is in the middle of Dongting Lake, the second largest freshwater lake in China," she says, her face bright with enthusiasm. "It is a place so beautiful that the very sight of it will make you forget your troubles."

The next day we take Sharon's advice. To get to Junshan Island, which is 10 miles from Yueyang, we have to take a ferry. However, when we get to the ferry dock, which is crowded with sampans, Sharon sweeps us aboard a small motor launch that would normally seat a half-dozen people comfortably. Here in China, however, 21 bodies are crammed into every available space; seven or eight intrepid daredevils even hang from the bow and sides of the vessel.

Nervously we peer into the water, which seems to be quite shallow, judging by the bamboo poles standing upright every 800 yards or so. The lack of depth comforts us somewhat, especially when we notice that there are no life jackets on board. Somehow we get under way, but not before the engine stalls thanks to the weight of too many passengers. And, as we slowly move through the muddy water to Junshan Island, we watch enviously as the ferry sails past us.

Junshan is quite small but, Sharon tells us, 10,000 troops still managed to live on it during the Song dynasty. We smile. After our boat trip to the island, we can appreciate crowding. Legend says that an emperor in ancient times toured the south and passed away not far from Yueyang. The emperor's two concubines followed their "husband" and arrived on Junshan Island, where they received the news of his death. They were so sad that they cried for a whole day, and while they cried they clutched at nearby bamboo stalks, staining the shafts with their tears. From that day on Junshan Island became the only place in the world where tearstained bamboo grows.

Junshan once boasted numerous temples, tombs, and pavilions, but only a dozen or so still exist, including the supposed grave of the famous grieving concubines. Swans, wild geese, cuckoos, and golden pheasants make the island a bird lover's paradise, and in Junshan's mountain streams the extremely rare golden turtle can be found by those with a great deal of patience. Even the so-called seven needles tea that grows here is unique. It has an unusual fragrance and its needles stand upright in a cup when hot water is poured on them.

Despite the blistering heat, Sharon continues to be effervescent, although her charges are noticeably wilting. As we totter along a concrete path, we nearly crash into a large camel, the last thing we expect to encounter. A little farther on we spot a go-cart track. Finally we arrive at the island's gift store where we barely have enough time to quench our thirst with warm colas.

Someone has bought a plastic battery-operated Buddha, which laughs hysterically and rocks back and forth when wound up. The Buddha's shrill laughter fills our motor launch as we head back to the Yueyang dock. "Is it not so?" Sharon asks, cutting through the inappropriate guffawing. "Has not Junshan's beauty made you forget your troubles?"

Yes, we all seem to be thinking as we smile, knowing the beauty of China still shines through all the claptrap. And maybe, after all, the plastic Buddha's hilarity isn't all that inappropriate. The lake and the island really have charmed us and stripped us of our cares, at least momentarily, as we watch the huddled buildings of Yueyang grow ever larger in front of us.

A dragon adorns one of the many temples found on Junshan Island.

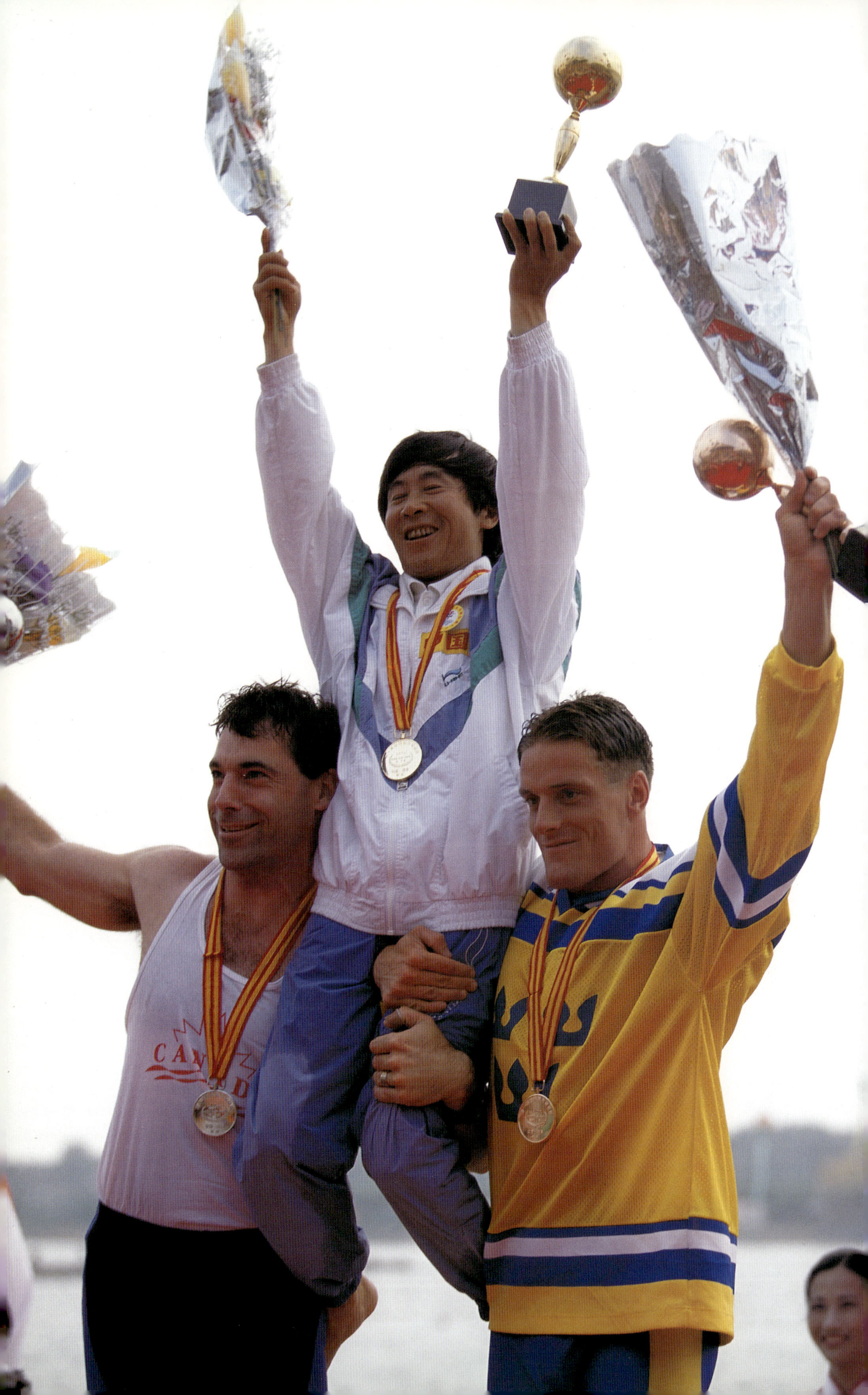

5 A Glorious Future

Dragon Boat Fever in the Next Millennium

As the dragon boat approaches the 550-meter mark in the race, the drummer and steersperson lock eyes momentarily. No words are spoken, but the drummer takes this as his cue to make a move. The team in the next boat has paddled stroke for stroke with them for the entire race and have now started to inch ahead with every pull. "No way!" says the drummer out loud. Then, glancing behind to confirm the location of the finish line, he raises one arm and calls out, "Finish in three, two, one!" In a split second the stroke rate jumps to an astonishing 118 strokes per minute, and within 10 strokes they have reasserted their lead. Victory will now taste even sweeter.

Stand before it and there is no beginning.
Follow it and there is no end.
Stay with the ancient Tao,
Move with the present.

ALL OVER THE WORLD dragon boat fever has gripped countries far removed from the sport's hotbeds in Hong Kong, Singapore, and China. Phenomenally places such as London, Stockholm, Rome, Berlin, Auckland, Sydney, New York, Boston, Dubuque, Seattle, Vancouver, Calgary, and Toronto have become passionate about an activity that likely owes its existence to the suicide of a Chinese poet-philosopher more than two millennia ago.

Every year dragon boat races spring up in new and unexpected countries like South Africa, Spain, Norway, and Holland, while event organizers have seen festivals double in size from year to year. And if the incredible development of festivals in Vancouver and Toronto or the intense racing fervor of New Zealand and Sweden are any indication, the world is in for some exciting racing in the near future.

Noting the worldwide growth in popularity of dragon boating, various dragon boat associations around the globe formed the International Dragon Boat Federation in 1991. The federation sees its chief role as "encouraging the development of the sport of dragon boat racing, and of maintaining its Asian cultural, historical, and religious traditions."

The victors in the mixed team 250-meter final in Yueyang in 1995: China (gold), Canada (silver), and Sweden (bronze).

> ### Yan Yan Li, *Hong Kong*
>
> Yan Yan started her paddling career in 1987 in Vancouver, British Columbia, with a mixed team called Aspirations, and later with the False Creek women's team (1989–1990). In November 1990 she moved to Hong Kong where she has paddled with both the Canadian Club of Hong Kong and the Hong Kong Island Paddle Club.
>
> In describing the races in Hong Kong in 1995, Yan Yan says, "It was a bit emotional and nerve-racking sitting at the start line sandwiched between False Creek on one side and Shun De on the other. It also makes me feel particularly proud of our team, which lacked the experience of the other international teams but was able to earn the privilege to compete in the same race."
>
> As she approaches her ninth year in dragon boating, Yan Yan says it is the "camaraderie that evolves out of dragon boating as well as the diversity, particularly in Hong Kong, of the people involved that keeps me going in the sport. Having everyone working together as one to achieve that perfect stroke, that perfect form, that perfect race is very rewarding. The greatest feeling in dragon boat racing, for sure, is when you hit that 'high' of 22 people working all-out, completely in sync, everyone focusing on one thing – victory."
>
> Yan Yan has raced in Vancouver, Singapore, Hong Kong, Bangkok, and various locations in China, including Beijing. Her team is made up of mostly expatriates from Canada, the United States, England, and Australia. They train in dragon boats, but they also use outrigger canoes that they had specially shipped from Vancouver. Yan Yan says she "got into paddling because it gives you an opportunity to get out on the water. It lets you escape."

Another of the federation's goals is to "promote and develop the sport and strengthen the bonds of friendship that unite those who practice it."

Lately the IDBF has mounted a campaign to convince the organizers of the Summer Olympic Games to recognize dragon boating as an official sport. If the People's Republic of China had won its bid for the Olympics in 2000, dragon boat racing, along with table tennis, would have been included as a demonstration sport. Sydney, Australia, however, was awarded the 2000 Olympics, and though interest in dragon boating is particularly high down under, the IDBF will probably have to wait until at least the 2004 Olympics to achieve its dream of demonstration status.

What kind of case can one make for the inclusion of dragon boating as an Olympic sport? First, it has a fair representation around the world now that 29 countries on five continents are registered with the IDBF. Second, many more countries hold dragon boat races and will no doubt soon be added to the IDBF's membership roll. Third, the IDBF is methodically organizing high-caliber international competitions on a regular basis. Fourth, dragon boating is an exciting sport to watch and would certainly be a crowd pleaser, something the International Olympic Committee (IOC) has definitely noticed.

A GLORIOUS FUTURE

Mike Haslam, president of the IDBF, has been a key player in pushing for Olympic recognition of dragon boating, and he is as optimistic as he is realistic about the sport's chances. Haslam says he is taking things "step by step" and adds, "Even if the Olympic Games approved dragon boating as a sport tomorrow, we'd still need 50 countries in the IDBF for the committee to accept our application. So we still have a long way to go." Toward that purpose, Haslam is excited about the fact that Penang, Malaysia, will stage a "Commonwealth Dragon Boat Championship" in conjunction with the 1998 Commonwealth Games, and hopes that Australia will hold a similar festival prior to its Olympics in 2000 which, auspiciously, is the Chinese year of the dragon.

Haslam has also written to the IOC in Lucerne, Switzerland, in order to ensure that the International Canoe Federation (ICF) won't claim dragon boating as one of its canoeing sports. "What this will mean," says Haslam, "is that if we're accepted in the Olympics, we'll be classified as a sport all on our own."

There are, however, a number of factors that will require consideration before dragon boating will gain acceptance at the Olympic level: the degree and kind of organization at the national and international levels; crew composition and level of expertise; and the standardization of equipment, rules, and regulations.

At the moment there is a disconcerting array of organizations in many countries. For example, the United States has at least two organizations – the American Dragon Boat Association and the United States Dragon Boat Association – that claim "national" status, and a similar situation exists in Canada. Furthermore, dragon boat organizations in different countries often operate totally oblivious to one

---

Ahmadi Caniago, *Bandung, Indonesia*

Dragon boating in Indonesia has one aspect that makes it quite different from how the sport is practiced in other countries – it is more or less a professional pastime. As Ahmadi Caniago, one of the members of the 1995 gold medal team at the Hong Kong festival, says, "We take dragon boating seriously. It's our job for five months of the year. Our team follows a rigorous training regime involving paddling practices six times a week, combined with three weight workouts and three or more runs per week."

Caniago has been paddling with his team since the late 1980s and comments that, prior to a big international competition, the team participates in a seven-week training camp. All of this dedication has certainly paid off for Indonesia. The country's men's teams have won top honors in Hong Kong five times since 1989.

> ### Anne-Marie Nehring, *Vancouver, Canada*
>
> Anne-Marie Nehring started paddling in 1986 and describes her introduction to the sport as "a time in my life when I just really wanted to be involved with a team." She started out as a paddler on the False Creek women's team, then moved to the position of steersperson. In 1995, she says, she "completed the circle" by becoming the drummer for the False Creek mixed team.
>
> "I like to drum now," says Nehring of her renewed love of the sport. "Drummers have a unique responsibility on a dragon boat team. They must unite the team with their words of encouragement and link the team with a stroke-by-stroke physical reality of the race. In a sense, the drummer strives to keep a paddler's head in the clouds and his feet in the boat."
>
> From her experience in all three positions she says that "In order to perform at a level to win a gold medal each individual athlete and the team as a unit must fuse their physical, mental, and spiritual parts. The athlete must combine physical strength and flexibility with the mental tenacity to hang on when every straining muscle is screaming, 'I can't!' At the same time he or she must have the spiritual openness to move into that world of power beyond time and limitations."
>
> As a steersperson, Nehring finds Victoria Harbour at the Hong Kong festival to be the most challenging racecourse. Says Nehring: "In most races, and on flat water, the actual physical act of steering the boat is a relatively easy task. Hong Kong, with its rough water, unpredictable waves, and boat traffic, makes the job all-important."

another, although this problem is rapidly being rectified by the IDBF.

Drew Mitchell, science and medicine coordinator at the Sport Medicine Council of British Columbia in Vancouver, says, "There has been a clash of concepts in the sport at the club level alone, whereby the pursuit of excellence has conflicted with the cultural and traditional concepts of what dragon boating is." He also points out that, "Hosting a 22-person team will be an expensive endeavor that could be a negative factor for the IOC. However, as an exhibition sport, perhaps the Olympic Committee will let dragon boating in because the athletes have to pay their own way."

Many dragon boat festivals are based on the original Chinese traditions, and the organizers of such events would likely want to maintain the status quo. Anne Watson of the Victoria Dragon Boat Association in Melbourne, Australia, leaves no doubt about the matter: "Our association wishes to maintain the community spirit of the festival rather than allow it to develop into an all-out sport."

Crew composition and the level of expertise are also important factors in the quest for Olympic status. Many dragon boat competitors are drawn increasingly to the sport's mixed class division. Unfortunately, however, in paddling sports there is no co-ed division at the Olympic level. In fact, there are very few Olympic events that allow the mixing of the sexes, particularly in the case of team sports. Sadly, in Vancouver,

A GLORIOUS FUTURE

interest in the open and women's divisions of dragon boating has been declining in recent years, and the open division was actually abandoned altogether for the 1995 festival due to lack of entries. Furthermore, the Vancouver festival had no division for women until 1990. Before that time women had to race in the mixed category. The 20 airline tickets to Hong Kong that were once awarded to the men's team (and later split with the women) used to attract a larger number of paddlers, but now the prizes are given only in the mixed division.

"The interest lies predominantly in the competitive mixed class in Vancouver," says Alison Hart, longtime member of the False Creek women's team. "Because the sport requires so many bodies, there is a real social component to it." Hart predicts this social component of the mixed division will be the "wave of the future."

Others such as Olympic gold medalist Hugh Fisher have another view of dragon boating's future. Fisher feels that the Olympics would be a sterile place for dragon boating, a sport that is steeped in tradition. "Every sport seems to strive to get into the Olympics," explains Fisher. "If dragon boating gets in, though, it will just be one more water event that uses neat-looking equipment."

Fisher sees dragon boating's greatest value as an entry-level activity for kids and as an introduction for them to the world of paddling sports. As he puts it, "Dragon boating is an excellent sport for its drawing

Iain Fisher, *Vancouver, Canada*

Iain Fisher has paddled dragon boats since 1986 and describes his move from competitive white-water canoeing to dragon boat racing as a "natural progression." He says he loves the competition and fitness that dragon boating provides and especially loves the travel. As part of the False Creek Men's Dragon Boat Team, Fisher has found himself competing all over Southeast Asia, Canada, and the United States.

When asked which race is his favorite, Fisher says he loves the competition in Hong Kong but was particularly impressed with the races and the venue in Yueyang. "We really didn't know what to expect when we went to Yueyang," says Fisher, a teacher in the Vancouver area. Before going, he asked some of his students whose parents were from China where Yueyang was, but nobody had ever heard of the place. "We figured we were going into the middle of nowhere, so we were quite surprised by the facilities."

In describing the opening ceremonies in Yueyang, Fisher says he was truly awed by the "sheer number" of people walking down to the race site. "It was like the whole world was walking with you!" he exclaims. "And everyone was so damn friendly."

Fisher adds that he would like to take his wife, Jennifer, and his two children, Neil and Angus, over to China someday. "Being in Hong Kong in 1997 would also be pretty exciting," he adds. "I think I might have to hold out for that. But then being in Australia for the year 2000 and the year of the dragon would also be pretty special!"

power, and dragon boats are great for paddling in all kinds of water conditions." The champion kayaker further believes the sport should look to places like New Zealand, a country where dragon fever has grown at a tremendous rate. He thinks this is partially due to the fact that New Zealanders have developed a boat that is both lightweight (500 pounds) and inexpensive (under CDN $5,000). "Obviously this makes the sport more affordable," he points out.

In any consideration of dragon boating as an Olympic event, the standardization of equipment and racecourses, as well as rules and regulations, ultimately becomes another major concern. Currently, as can be seen in the survey of dragon boat festivals around the world in chapter 4, there is a plethora of course distances, boat types, and rules even in the same country.

However, the second IDBF Congress, held in 1993, did agree in principle that "from the year 2000 the Hong Kong design of the dragon boat will be the standard boat for use in IDBF Championship Regattas." Traditional teak boats vary in weight from one craft to the next (sometimes by more than 100 pounds), so it seems only fair to assume that fiberglass boats, which are more consistent in weight, not to mention far less expensive, should be considered in the selection of a standard boat type. And finally there is the question of the dragon boat's general design. The Hong Kong-designed teak boat is more suited to smaller, lighter East Asian teams, and perhaps the IDBF should insist on setting a standard that falls between the teak model and the fiberglass variant.

Should the IDBF continue with its drive to gain Olympic status it

---

Verna Okell, Portland, *Oregon, U.S.A.*

Verna Okell has paddled with Mountain Home Canoe since the early 1990s and currently acts as a stroke for the boat on the right side. She has raced in Portland, Seattle, Dubuque, Lake Tahoe, Los Angeles, Vancouver, and Calgary, but admits that winning in Seattle was a highlight for her. "It's exciting to see that festival double in size since last year [1994]," she enthuses. "Seattle's races have a great future. The boats are faster and sleeker than ours and that makes for more competition and excitement."

Okell finds Portland's heavy ceremonial boats much more difficult to paddle, but relief is on the way. "We now have new North American-style fiberglass boats to train in, which means there will be even more racing in Portland."

The Portland native's favorite festival, however, is Vancouver's, although she also has a soft spot for the racing events that take place up and down the Mississippi. What does she love most about dragon boating? "Definitely the team spirit," she replies. "There's nothing like it."

A GLORIOUS FUTURE

> ### Carlos Capdevila, *Burlington, Iowa, U.S.A.*
>
> For nearly a decade Carlos Capdevila has been the steersperson for Burlington's Budragons, which is also one of the chief organizers of the town's dragon boat festival. "Dragon boating," he says, "is one of the few sports you can really get into regardless of age and still feel like a competitor." Capdevila thinks the recreational aspect of the Burlington races, which take place on the Mississippi River, is what makes his hometown's festival so popular. "Of course," he adds, "our parties are really incredible, too. We put as much work into the social events as we do into the races."
>
> Burlington's festival features a "buddy team" that serves as the host team for out-of-town crews. "I've seen teams that have been here only two days that leave crying. We get really serious on the water and then we're brothers and sisters again." The Burlington Dragon Boat Festival's motto is FRIENDSHIP THROUGH PADDLING, which is obviously something this Midwest American town doesn't take lightly.

will have to grapple with certain contradictions inherent in its own objectives. Can the federation rationalize its own stated desire "to protect and maintain the Asian cultural, historical, and religious traditions of dragon boat racing" while achieving the kind of standardization of equipment, rules, and racecourses necessary for Olympic and Commonwealth recognition?

It is doubtful that, on the Olympic level at least, such religious and cultural traditions would be allowed. Many sports such as hockey, baseball, and basketball had their origins in specific countries, namely Canada and the United States, but at the international level they carry absolutely no cultural accoutrements. Russians and Italians can play hockey as if they invented it, just as Cubans and Japanese can excel at baseball as if it had always been a mainstay of their cultures. But can South Africa and Sweden compete in dragon boating at the Olympic level with all of the Chinese ceremony and tradition still attached? Undoubtedly this question may prove to be the most vexing one for the IDBF in its pursuit of the ultimate international status.

While there are individuals and groups striving for standardization, other dragon boat enthusiasts prize the sport's diversity. To such

> ### Eve Glinow, *Liverpool, England*
>
> Eve Glinow was first introduced to dragon boating during a charity event. After being diagnosed with terminal breast cancer a few years ago, she was urged by her partner, Andy Pearson, to continue dragon boating as a way of staying healthy and fit. Glinow managed to squeeze in workouts between nursing shifts, and "miraculously," she says, "the cancer went into remission." After racing in Hong Kong, the British Royal Marines team found itself short a few paddlers, and Glinow soon found herself paddling with a mostly male crew.
>
> What she finds most appealing about the sport is that "You don't have to be a great athlete to take up paddling a dragon boat. Anyone with the motivation can do it. It's a sport that requires cooperation rather than isolation."

> ### Uta Schoppe, *Dresden, Germany*
> Uta Schoppe has been paddling dragon boats for a Dresden team since 1991. Of all the races she has participated in since, Schoppe found her first exposure to the festival in Yueyang, China, to be the most unique. "The people, the town, the country, everything was so exciting," she enthuses.
> "Dragon boat racing," she says, "has grown rapidly in Germany. Now there are festivals in Dresden, Berlin, Hamburg, Frankfurt, Rostock, Hannover, Wuppertal, and Schwerin." Both teak and fiberglass boats, as well as vessels from Taiwan and Singapore, are used in Germany. Schoppe expects dragon boating to become an even bigger sport in Germany over the next few years, particularly with the Eurocup competition that pits Germany against England, Norway, Sweden, Italy, Holland, Belgium, and many other Europeans countries.

people the ability to rise to the challenge of longer or shorter race distances, lighter or heavier boats, rougher or calmer waters is part of the challenge and excitement that make dragon boating so attractive. If a sport can be said to have a period of innocence, it can also be said that such innocence begins to crumble when that sport starts to codify its rules and regulations.

Regardless of what lies ahead, however, one thing is certain: dragon boating is truly a celebration! The sport, which at one time was little known beyond the borders of China, has brought together thousands of people from all over the world in friendship and friendly competition. On the water it is a test of strength, stamina, and commitment to a team no matter what level of skill a participant may have. Off the water it is a festival rich in traditions that date back more than 2,000 years.

So for those who have never picked up a paddle, contact your local dragon boating club or federation for information on joining a team. But be careful . . . you will almost certainly find the sport addictive!

> ### Kurt Hill, *Sydney, Australia*
> Kurt Hill's Port Hacking Dragon Boat Club was first established in 1983. The following year the team won the inaugural Australian Dragon Boat Races in Sydney, and later that same year it made quite a splash in Singapore and Hong Kong.
> Since then, Hill says, the team has been a mainstay at festivals and races in Australia and the Far East. Other teams from down under, such as the Fremantle Swan Dragon Boat Club men's and women's teams, have also had great success internationally.
> Hill points to the superb organizational structure of Australian dragon boating as one of the chief reasons for its rapid growth. His own state organization, Dragon Boats New South Wales, is instrumental in staging the Sydney Dragon Boat Festival annually, and each state in Australia has a similar association overseeing the sport.

August Betham, *Wellington, New Zealand*

August Betham has been paddling since the early 1990s with the New Zealand national team. When asked about how he got involved in the sport, he says he went to watch a dragon boat race in Wellington and was immediately captivated by the sight of it.

Betham admits that he didn't pursue the sport until his wife, Tracy, added his name to a list for new recruits put up by a local dragon boat team. After his first training run, though, he knew he was hooked. Says Betham: "I just loved the sport from the time I had a paddle in my hand."

After seeing New Zealand's national team practicing, Betham knew he wanted to become involved at a higher level. Fortunately for him, a local radio station announced that the team was looking for "experienced" paddlers, and after a "few white lies," Betham found himself in the team's boat.

He explains that he sees dragon boating as a sport that has allowed his family to be involved. "It's taken me to a lot of places, first around New Zealand and now around the world. I've made a lot of new friends."

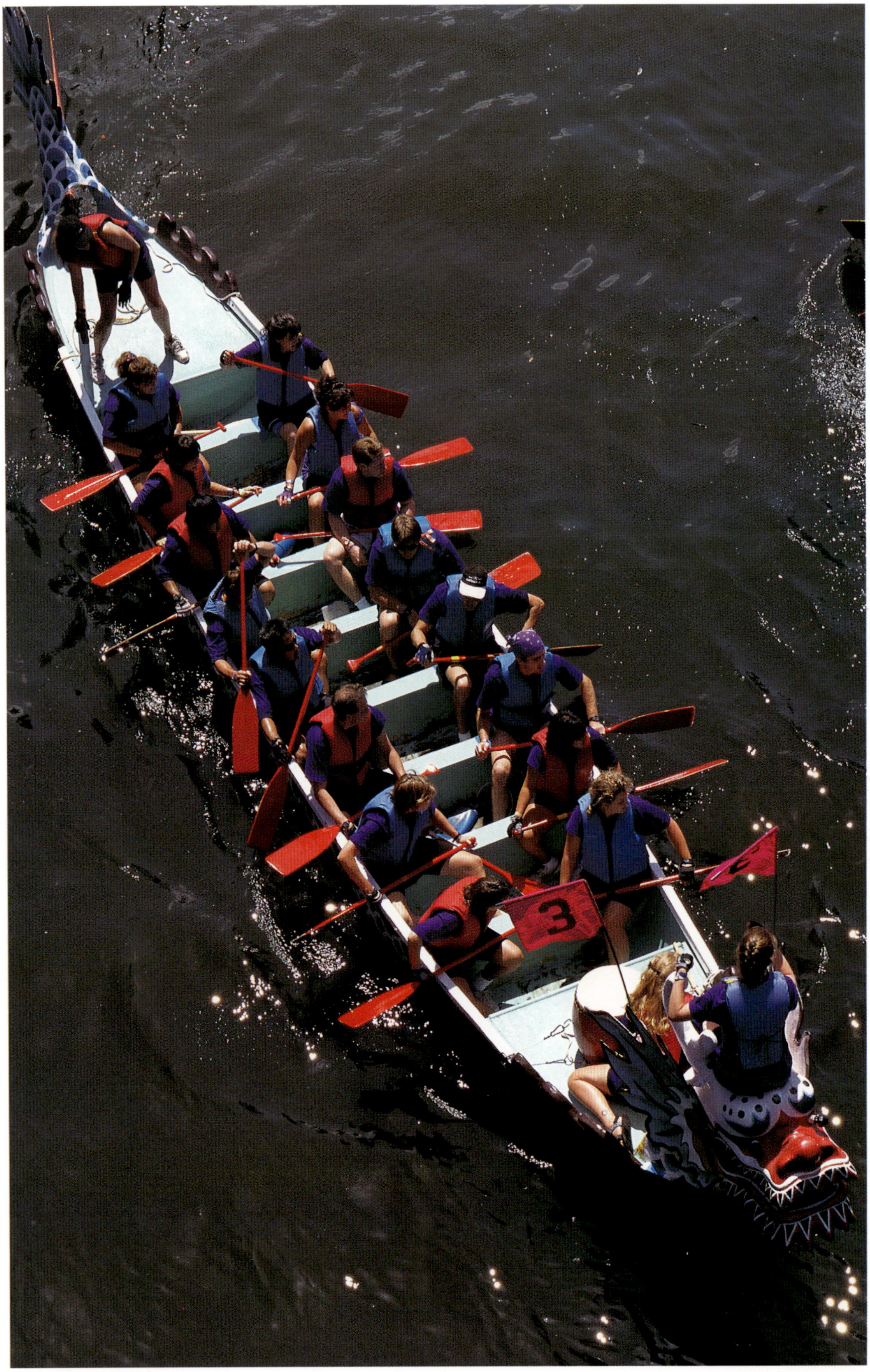

Glossary

BACK PADDLING: the stroke used in paddling sports to bring a boat backward into or away from a loading dock or a race start.

BILGE: the part of the underwater body of a boat between the flat of the bottom and the vertical topsides.

BOW: the front of a boat. In a dragon boat the drummer is the person closest to the bow, which is also known as the prow.

BREASTHOOK: a steel plate or timber in the form of a knee secured internally across the stem of a vessel to add strength to its structure.

BULKHEAD: an upright partition in a boat separating compartments or areas.

CATCH: the third element of the dragon boat stroke and the point when the paddle blade first comes into contact with the water.

DRAW STROKE: stroke used most often by front or back paddlers to line up a boat straight at the start line of a race or to turn a boat around.

CHINE: the intersection of the bottom and the sides of a flat or V-bottomed boat.

COXSWAIN: a steersperson in a racing boat who usually directs paddlers or rowers.

DRUMMER: the person who sets a dragon boat crew's timing by rhythmically pounding a drum. The drummer sits in the bow and is usually lightweight (90 to 125 pounds).

EVEN KEEL: see TRIM.

EXIT: the fifth element of the dragon boat stroke in which the paddle leaves the water cleanly and quickly midway between the paddler's knee and hip.

DRAGON BOATS: A CELEBRATION

FAIRINGS: removable brackets on a teak dragon boat to which the dragon's head and tail are attached.

FAN: a construction consisting of five wedges of wood scarfed together at both ends of a teak dragon boat. In a fiberglass dragon boat the fans are purely decorative, but in a teak boat the fans are attached to the keelson and help prevent the vessel from buckling in the middle.

FIGUREHEAD: an ornamental carved and painted figure located at the bow of a boat, generally expressing some aspect of the boat's name or function.

FINISH: the point near the end of a dragon boat race when a team's drummer calls for a crew's stroke rate to be increased.

FREEBOARD: the distance between the waterline and the upper edge of the side of a boat. A loss of freeboard is the most common reason for a dragon boat to sink.

FU ZHOU: paper bills used in dragon boat festival ceremonies.

GUNWALE: the upper edge of a boat's side.

HAKA: traditional Maori war dance.

HULL: the frame or body of a boat exclusive of masts, yards, sails, and rigging.

HUN: in Chinese folk belief, the spirit of a person or thing.

114

GLOSSARY

KEEL: the chief structural member of a boat that extends longitudinally along the center of its bottom and that often projects from the bottom.

KNEE: a timber or metal bar fashioned into a right angle to provide strengthening and support at the intersections of a vessel's framework.

KEELSON: a longitudinal structure running above and fastened to the keel of a boat in order to stiffen and strengthen the framework.

NAGA: a snakelike creature in East Indian mythology similar to the Chinese dragon.

PORT: the left side of a boat looking forward. Also called larboard.

PRY STROKE: stroke used by paddlers to line up a boat or to draw a boat over to one side. Also called a PUSHAWAY STROKE.

PULL: the fourth element of the dragon boat stroke in which the paddle is fully buried in the water and the paddler pulls water back toward himself or herself directly parallel with the boat.

REACH/EXTENSION: the second element of the dragon boat stroke in which the paddler maximizes the length of his or her stroke before plunging the blade of the paddle into the water.

RECOVERY: the final element of the dragon boat stroke in which the racer's paddle has left the water and is snapped forward just before it enters the water again to begin another stroke sequence.

ROCKER: either of two curving pieces of wood or metal on which an object rocks.

ROTATION: the first element in the dragon boat stroke in which the paddler achieves sufficient torso rotation so that reach/extension, the next element in the stroke, can be maximized.

RUSHING: what occurs when a dragon boat paddler's timing is ahead of and out of sync with the rest of a boat's crew.

SCARF: a joint made by chamfering, halving, or notching two pieces to correspond and then lapping or bolting them. Often called a scarf joint. TO SCARF means to unite by a scarf joint.

SKYING: a flaw in dragon boat technique in which a paddler lifts the paddle blade too high out of the water during the recovery phase of the stroke.

STARBOARD: the right side of a boat looking forward.

STEM: the foremost timber or steel member forming the bow of a vessel joined at the bottom to the keel either by scarfing or riveting.

STERN: the rear end of a boat.

STEERSPERSON: the person located at the stern of a dragon boat who is responsible for steering the boat and encouraging the crew.

STROKE: refers to the technique of bringing a dragon boat paddle into, through, and out of the water. Also refers to the two paddlers in the first seat of a boat who work with the drummer to set the pace for the rest of the team.

STROKE RATE: the paddling pace in a dragon boat; the number of times the paddle goes through the water per minute. The usual racing rate for competitive teams is about 82 strokes per minute.

THOLE: wooden pin(s) fixed close together in a block of wood to keep the steering oar in place while steering.

THWART: a rower or paddler's seat placed across a boat.

TOPSIDES: the part of a vessel that is above the main wales.

TRIM: the way a boat sits in the water while floating. When properly trimmed, a boat should sit level.

WALE: an extra thickness of wood bolted to the sides of a vessel in positions where protection is needed.

ZONG ZI: rice dumplings made popular by the legend of the renowned Chinese poet, Qu Yuan. A culinary staple at most dragon boat festivals.

Bibliography

Bassett, Fletcher S. *Legends and Superstitions of the Sea and of Sailors.* Detroit: Detroit Singing Tree Press, 1971.

Berliner, Nancy Zeng. *Chinese Folk Art.* Boston: Little, Brown, 1986.

Best, Elsdon. *The Maori Canoe.* Wellington, NZ: A. R. Shearer, Government Printer, 1976.

Bodde, Derk. *Festivals in Classical China.* Princeton, NJ: Princeton University Press, 1975.

Brewington, M.V. *Shipcarvers of North America.* New York: Dover Publications, 1972.

Bringhurst, Robert. *The Black Canoe.* Vancouver: Douglas and McIntyre, 1991.

Churbuck, D. C. *The Book of Rowing.* Woodstock, NY: Overlook Press, 1988.

Cooper, J. C. *An Illustrated Encyclopedia of Traditional Symbols.* London: Thames and Hudson, 1987.

Dyson, George. *Baidarka.* Edmonds, WA: Alaska Northwest, 1986.

Dyson, Verne. *Forgotten Tales of Ancient China.* Shanghai: Commercial Press, 1934.

Encyclopedia of Magic and Superstition. London: Macdonald and Company, 1988.

Gerr, Dave. *The Nature of Boats.* Camden, ME: International Marine, 1992.

Hansen, Hans Jurgen. *Art and the Seafarer.* New York: Viking, 1968.

The Hawaiian Canoe. Hanalei, HI: Tommy Holmes Editions, 1981.

Hawkes, David. *Ch'u Tz'u: The Songs of the South*. London: Oxford University Press, 1959.

Hodous, Lewis. *Folkways in China*. London: Arthur Probsthain, 1929.

Hoult, Janet. *Dragons: Their History and Symbolism*. Glastonbury, Eng.: Gothic Image Publications, 1987.

Hucker, Charles O. *China's Imperial Past: An Introduction to Chinese History and Culture*. Stanford, CA: Stanford University Press, 1975.

Huxley, Francis. *The Dragon: Nature of Spirit, Spirit of Nature*. London: Thames and Hudson, 1989.

Kemp, Peter, ed. *The Oxford Companion to Ships and the Sea*. Oxford: Oxford University Press, 1995.

Kentley, Eric. *Boat*. Don Mills, ON: Stoddart, 1992.

Kranz, Jacqueline L. *American Nautical Art and Antiques*. New York: Crown, 1981.

Lao Tsu. *Tao Te Ching*. Trans. Gia-Fu Feng and Jane English. New York: Vintage, 1989. All uncredited epigraphs in *Dragon Boats* have been taken from this translation.

Lawson, Thomas. *Chinese Art of the Warring States Period*. Washington, DC: Smithsonian Institution, 1982.

Leach, Maria, ed. *Funk & Wagnalls Standard Dictionary of Folklore, Mythology, and Legend*. New York: Harper and Row, 1984.

Lim, Liliane Kim. *The Chinese Dragon*. Hong Kong: Pencoed Ltd., 1987.

Mason, Bill. *The Path of the Paddle*. Toronto: Van Nostrand Reinhold, 1980.

Nelson, Anne. *Nga Waka Maori: Maori Canoes*. Auckland, NZ: Macmillan, 1991.

Orlick, Terry. *In Pursuit of Excellence: How to Win in Sport and Life Through Mental Training*. Champaign, IL: Leisure Press, 1990.

Roberts, Kenneth G. and Philip Shackleton. *The Canoe: A History of the Craft from Panama to the Arctic*. Toronto: Macmillan, 1983.

Rosenthal, Doris, comp. *Pertaining to Boats*. New York: Brown-Robertson, 1928.

BIBLIOGRAPHY

Shi, Cang, ed. *The Dragon*. Beijing: People's Daily Press, 1988.

Vocino, Michele. *Ships Through the Ages*. Milan: Edizioni Luigi Alfieri, 1951.

Watson, Burton. *Early Chinese Literature*. New York: Columbia University Press, 1962.

Wiley, Jack. *How to Build Your Own Fiberglass Hull or Kit*. Lodi, CA: Solipaz Publishing Company, 1991.

Wong, C. S. *A Cycle of Chinese Festivals*. Singapore: Malaysia Publishing House, 1967.

Xin, Yang, Li Yihau and Xu Naixiang. *The Art of the Dragon*. Hong Kong: Commercial Press, 1988.

Illustration Credits

PAT BARKER: pages 11, 12, 53, 54, and 80.

YUN LAM LI: pages 15, 28, 29, 31, 34, 35, 52, and 90.

ROD LUEY: pages 6, 49, 78, 79, 86, and 112.

PAUL MORRISON: pages ii, vi, viii, x, xii, xvi, xviii, 2, 4, 5, 7, 9, 10, 13, 16, 17, 18, 20, 36, 38, 40, 43, 46, 47, 48, 51, 57, 58, 59, 61, 62, 63, 66, 68, 69, 70, 71, 72, 74, 82, 83, 85, 88, 93, 96, 97, 101, 102, 104, 105, 106, 107, 108, and 111.

BOB SOLAR: page 114.

JIM SOLAR: pages 24, 25, 32, 33, and 65.

JEFF VINNICK: page 44.